Love and Merry Christmas

About the Stories

Jingle Bell Bodyguard by Christine Wingate
Harper Palmquist has been quietly drooling over gym hottie Rick Avery
every Saturday. Can a series of mishaps over a Christmas season create
the perfect setting for romance?

Home for Christmas by Susan Craig
Max Moretti has long treasured memories of a beautiful red-haired
woman from his past. When fate brings her into his life together again,
can he convince April they can create a new home…together?

Christmas a La by Jeanne Kern
Stressed-out Susan Albright is overwhelmed about hosting her family for
Christmas. Hiring fortune teller Zelda seems like the perfect way to get
everyone the right gift. But the mysterious lady just might have enough
magic left over to arrange a surprise for her.

The Christmas Gift by BJ Akin
Young Sandhills teacher, Miss Rebecca, faces the raging storm on an
untamed Nebraska prairie with courage. She's concerned for the welfare
of two particular students, and ends up with more than she bargained for
when their widowed father comes to her aid.

Starstruck by LK Lien
When a bright new star appears in the sky, it is only the beginning of the
miracle season. But closed hearts resist miracles. It takes a lot of love
wrapped with a blast of fun to break through the barricades.

Blame it on the Christmas Lights by Karyn Cole
Lucy Potter isn't very thrilled with the start of her holiday season. She's
convinced her only long-term relationship will be with her favorite
sweatpants. But Christmas gets unexpectedly merry when she runs into
an old crush. Will she be able to enjoy the gifts of the season? Or will
thoughts of what might not be, ruin it all?

Table of Contents

Jingle Bell Bodyguard

By

Christine Wingate

Dear Reader:

Happy Holidays! Thanks for reading *Jingle Bell Bodyguard*. The most common question I get from those reading this selection is an easy one to answer. No, I've never ever been made aware of anyone being assaulted by jingle bells. Please know that I do not condone or encourage any such behavior, either. Antics like this are generally fun to read about *only*. Whew. Please know that you can read a bit more about some of the characters mentioned in a few other adventures within my other books. Check out www.christinewingate.com for the full scoop.

Warmest regards,
~ Christine

Rick Avery has very hot, sexy, manly legs.

I think this naughty thought as the object of my regular Saturday morning drool session walks by the machines where Ginger and I exercise.

We never speak to one another, Rick and I. Or nod our heads. We barely smile, even. I don't dare try as Rick and Ginger have some sort of past.

But his eyes always catch mine for a second longer than feels rational and electricity zings between us. My stomach does a quick back flip.

Then he passes me on those yummy legs -- and the moment is lost.

I could set a clock to the moment. Every Saturday morning. Exactly 9:56 a.m.

But drooling over Rick isn't the only reason I'm here. The front row of elliptical machines at the top floor of my health club is a great place to be with your best girlfriend on a cold Saturday morning. The hand-to-hand combat class starting soon in the room behind us has lots of attendees, so the room with the bikes, rowing machines and elliptical equipment in this outer area is almost always empty.

Which is what Ginger Burton and I need. We can kill the proverbial two birds with one stone. My best girlfriend and I can exercise *AND* have our weekly chat fest at the same time.

I mean, well, Ginger usually does most of the talking. I sort of toss out words in between laborious puffs of breath. Physical exertion is not really my thing. But I've been promoted to a retail shop manager in the past few months, and looking healthy and fit in my clothes is good for sales, and my commission bonuses. Oh. And I sort of guess exercise is good for my health, blah blah blah.

Either way, exercise counts, you know! Even if you breathe really hard during the activity. As an added bonus, after I endure the Saturday morning torture, I can justify enjoying one of those large macadamia and white chocolate cookies they sell at the snack bar downstairs on my way out.

Confession Moment: Sometimes I get two cookies. Hey, don't roll your eyes at me. The lady at the counter assures me they put protein powder in the cookies -- so it's like eating a healthy cookie and not just a straight indulgence. Protein powder is good for me...and it's not like I ASKED them to put it in a cookie. They came up with that idea. Although, I am grateful.

So, it's Saturday. Hottie Rick just walked by. I'm on my usual elliptical machine and already thinking about eating my beloved, perfectly crunchy macadamia nut cookie when Ginger drops me the latest love news. My world is steady and even and predictable.

"Henry is taking me to Hawaii for Christmas this year for my holiday present." Ginger manages to say the words smoothly and casually, despite the fact her legs are moving at warp speed on her machine.

A pang of happiness, then jealousy hits my chest.

Wha-huh?! Christmas is only a week away!

Play it cool, Harper, I tell myself.

"I thought…your enormous…diamond engagement ring…was your present this year," I huff, glancing only fleetingly at my best friend's hand. The square gem sparkles and shimmers impressively even in the harsh, unforgiving fluorescent light at the health club.

Ginger laughs. "Henry says he's been planning this for awhile. The original idea was that he would propose while we were in Hawaii. But once he got the ring, he couldn't wait."

"Ah. That's…romantic." It *is* romantic. At the same time, it's also inconvenient for the holiday plans Ginger and I had tentatively made.

Ginger presses a button on her machine and the speed of her pedals kicks up a notch. She's exercising on the fuel of happy adrenaline. Argh. It's official. I'm the worst friend in the world. I'm jealous of Ginger's boyfriend, her holiday plans…*and* her workout adrenaline.

I cringe and focus on my future cookie reward. *Mmmm. Cookie.*

Ginger is telling me the details, but I'm not really listening. Instead, I pretend to be thrilled for her and not sad for me.

My girlfriend's taut stomach muscles and toned arms gracefully glide into a new rhythm. One thing is for sure, well-toned Ginger will look beautiful in a swimsuit on the beach in the next week, and her Henry will be drooling when she struts her stuff atop the sand.

My best girlfriend is the whole package. Smart. Beautiful. Kind. Henry is a lucky guy.

There's a lull in the conversation and I'm afraid Ginger might figure out I've been lost in my own thoughts. I try to cover quickly.

"Won't you…miss all this…cold, snowy…Iowa weather?"

"Ha-ha."

"What about Christmas with your mother?"

She grins. "Know what, Harper? I'll have to sacrifice that crazy family dinner for love, this year. I'll bring her back something fancy and a pineapple and I'm sure she'll be happy as a clam."

Ginger starts to tell me about what she'll be packing on the trip. A new sarong. New sandals. Since she travels a lot for her job as a medical supply salesperson, she already has nearly everything she needs in her meticulously-arranged closet.

I half-listen, but my thoughts are on myself. With my parents going on their holiday cruise and my brother working overseas this year, Christmas is taking a grumpy-elf-sort-of-turn this season.

Henry's surprise is wonderful and romantic. But my de-facto Christmas plans with Ginger certainly won't be happening this year. *Bah-humbug.* Besides the fact that my job in the little mall boutique is crazy this time of year, being the manager requires I work nearly all shifts during Christmas. Bottom line…going with anyone on holiday trips isn't possible.

So with Ginger officially gushing about her plans, one thing is for certain. I'll be alone for the holiday this year.

Alone. Over Christmas. For the first time ever.

Double bah-humbug.

A pang of sadness and self-pity hits me full-force in the stomach. For the moment, of course, I blame exercise for the yucky feeling washing all over my body and keep my *'I'm thrilled for you'* face on for Ginger's benefit. I'll deal with reality later when I'm alone in my apartment.

Holidays haven't been my friend lately.

I managed to catch the stomach flu over Thanksgiving. Of course, that was a relatively minor disaster in terms of the emotional impact compared to the last day of October. When my boyfriend of 11 months, Travis, unceremoniously dumped me for my bikini waxer at my own Halloween party. An absolute downer.

Well, of course, I ultimately lost four pounds due to being sick over Thanksgiving. And that was kind of nice, in retrospect. But the three pounds I lost in tears crying over Travis was brutal on a visceral level.

Granted, Bikini Beth looked very sexy as a Nile Princess when she dropped into my bash unexpectedly. White, sleeveless dress. Sexy, long black hair in the wig. And don't forget the fancy gold crown.

Still, Travis and I had been dating for almost an entire year and he only spent a mere two hours chatting up Beth before he pulled me aside and let me know he was breaking up with me. I mean, *two hours!* What's up with that?

I should have known something was up when he kept replenishing Beth's vampire punch and gave her the very last ghost chocolate sandwich cookie.

Those clues were just the foreshadowing element that something at my party was slowly melting away, like the proverbial witch who's been doused with water.

No, my relationship with Travis wasn't officially over until I lost to Beth during the toilet paper zombie wrap game finals. I noticed how my boyfriend ignored me and went straight to lovingly peeling the double-ply tissue away from Beth's legs, waist and shoulders. Moments later, Travis broke up with me whilst I was stirring the salad with a creepy pair of skeleton-bone tongs.

Cowboy Travis rode off into the sunset with Nile Princess Beth five minutes later. Two minutes after that, I struggled maneuvering my little Bo Peep skirt into the laundry room down the hall from my apartment so I could have a good, proper cry in private. It was an especially messy cry since I'd had to steal all the toilet paper from everywhere for the zombie game to ensure we had enough.

Anyway, ugly emergency cry...no toilet paper. Insult to injury, as they say.

After a few weeks, though, another complication of Travis and Beth's new love connection reared its ugly head. Being dropped like last year's broken smoke machine was bad. But Beth had been giving me some of the best spa treatments I'd ever had. Turns out, finding a new competent waxing person became even more painful for me in another sort of way.

Now that the emotional pain had subsided, I found myself wondering -- did I miss Beth (the best bikini waxer in the world) more than I missed Travis (the inattentive but most handsome boyfriend I'd ever had?)

I was still deciding. That itself spoke volumes about how much I really liked Travis. But Travis was comfortable and we were well-suited. Or so I thought before my costume party and he wrangled another filly.

Ginger's laugh jolts my wandering mind back to the present.

I laugh, too. I've barely been paying attention and I think she's made a joke about Henry seducing her while he's wearing a grass skirt.

Ginger resumes talking. But I'm still thinking about what happens in a few short days.

Me. Alone. All Christmas Day.

I politely try to notch up my exercise speed. Might as well channel my frustration in a productive way. My leg muscles groan, but I try to ignore the pain.

"What are you doing on Christmas, then?"

I shrug and pretend like I haven't thought about it.

"I'll drink…loads of eggnog…and…watch lots of great…Christmas movies."

"I have a better idea for you." Ginger slides me a half smile. "And you need to listen before you label it 'stinky.' "

"Is it…stinky?"

"There are different forms of stinky, Harper."

"What?"

"There's a stinky as in I-forgot-to-water-all-my poinsettias-and-now-they-are-dead stinky." Ginger tilts her head to the side. "And there's a grown-men-dressed-as-mall-elves-are-trying-to pinch-my-butt-when-I-take-my-nieces-to-get-their-picture-taken-at-the-mall stinky."

"What's…the difference?"

"One is your own fault for not putting in the effort to make something flourish. The other we fault the universe for because despite your best efforts, the creepy results are what you seem to attract."

I turn my eyes away from Ginger's slyly accusing ones and focus back on the television screens bolted into the front walls.

Here we go again.

"You're getting ready…to pressure me again."

"Yes, I am." Ginger punches a button on her machine so that it goes even faster. Her perfect body picks up the pace. She looks like a graceful exercise commercial model. "Maybe now you'll let me set you up with one of the guys from my accounting division."

"No." I huff my answer quickly. And for good measure, I punch a button on my own machine up yet another notch. Now, I nearly match Ginger's speed. "You've set me up…with four…bad blind dates and…the fourth time was not a charm…and…I think…I would have to…get completely drunk on…high octane eggnog…before I…"

"I'm not taking 'no' for an answer." Ginger informs me. I sneak a sideways glance at her. Only a light, moist sheen of perspiration glistens on her face. She's dabbing at her neck with a pristine white towel. "If you don't have a date on Christmas Eve, then you have to let me set you up with Charlie."

I gasp. "Charlie Nashton?" My eyes narrow. "You wouldn't!"

"I would." Ginger stubbornly squints back. "He a nice guy and he's been very interested in you for weeks. Every Tuesday afternoon he stops by my office and asks about you. "

"No!" I shake my head vigorously. "I've told you…before. I cannot …date a man who has…rigid routines like that. I'd probably slip…into insanity after two weeks…and bludgeon the poor man to death with his…giant solar accounting calculator."

"A date is better than no date, Harper." Ginger is playing dirty now. "Besides, I'm not leaving for a Christmas holiday knowing you're alone. If Charlie is the only option, then I'm setting you up and there's nothing you can do--"

"Maybe I could help out with that." A deep, rich voice from just behind me cuts Ginger off. "Hey, Harper."

Instinctively, I immediately turn to the source. I half-turn and recognize the legs immediately – even if I can't place the voice.

Hottie Rick Avery. Gym hottie. Bodyguard. Guy who stars in all my fantasy boyfriend daydreams.

He smiles at me. Is he flirting with me? I'd be at risk at drooling back at him in reply if I wasn't totally out of breath.

The realization that Rick is, indeed, grinning at me seems to affect my nervous system with an unfortunate chain reaction. My hands loosen on the moving handles. My legs suddenly forget they are supposed to keep moving at this unfamiliar warp speed. My foot catches awkwardly on the step. Before I know what's happening, I'm airborne. Flying backwards, propelled by a flying arm handle.

I'm slow-motion flying for a millisecond. I'm soaring. I see Ginger gasp, but I don't hear the sound associated with the effort. Intellectually, my brain tells me I'll be connecting with the floor in a moment. I brace for impact.

Two strong hands pluck me from my inadvertent flight. My shoulder hits a rock-hard chest. My forehead rubs against a deliciously-stubbled chin. I inhale the distinctive scent of leather, coffee and man.

Eyes closed, I draw in the sexy smell of Rick. It's better than I imagined. There's a solid warm body pressed up against me and I lean into the sensation. It occurs to me that I may have been knocked unconscious and am only dreaming. Who cares? This hallucination is crazy fabulous and I never want it to end. Rick Avery's fantastically sexy voice is even whispering in my ear.

"Whoa. Gotcha."

Rick Avery has me. His voice even implies he doesn't mind!

Yep. I've got to be dreaming. In real life, Rick Avery may well be horrified at my inadvertent acrobatics…but in my concussed alternate world, he's nice, solid-yet-cuddly and smells nice.

Rick Avery has very hot, sexy, manly arms.

I let myself linger in the mirage I don't want to end. Ever.

Funny. The goosebumps erupting everywhere on my body even feel real. Why do concussions get such a bad rap, I wonder? Hmmm. Head doctors probably don't want it getting out how some such injuries have such nice side effects when it comes to dreamy fantasies. People would probably run off and start wonking themselves in the head all the time. Can't have that. Society would fall apart.

But, surely, no one could really blame me if I were to hit myself in the head only once more later after this one wears off.

Just one more smack and I could have enough delight to last for a really long while.

I flutter my eyes a bit, ready to advance to the visual part of my dream. My ponytail hair is partially covering my face and I can't easily see any of Rick's gorgeously masculine face. Or admire his broad shoulders.

Some of the flopped hair attaches to my tongue because my mouth is slightly open. I blink. And flutter my tongue to push the strands away.

It's another full three or four seconds -- maybe longer -- before it occurs to me that perhaps I am not truly concussed. Tentatively, I move my hand to brush my ponytail away from its backwards summersault drape over my face.

When I do this, I'm truly rewarded. A very handsome, completely unshaken Rick Avery face staring down at me.

He's grinning and my stomach does a little flip.

He speaks first. "You okay?"

"I'm...great." My voice is a whisper that's uncharacteristically breathy. I may even sound a bit like Marilyn Monroe.

Rick's eyes peer down on me. They are even more beautiful than that time he looked at me that one time we were simultaneously at the drinking fountain.

Rick Avery has very hot, sexy, manly eyes.

"You heard her. She's great. Let her go, already."

Why does the Ginger in my dreams have to be so much like the real-life Ginger and cross with Rick all the time? My dreamy Rick, though, doesn't make a move to remove me from his grasp. I look elsewhere and try to focus my vision. Why do I still have leg cellulite? Why am I not wearing something sexier?

Uh-oh.

I freeze. You know, if I were truly someone Rick had recently rescued from an elliptical machine…well, this moment could actually be…honestly, more than a little embarrassing.

My arms and legs respond awkwardly to my silent commands to move. All parts of my body with muscles and bones have been jellified. By the mind-numbing dream yumminess of Rick Avery.

Or from the insane workout tempo and/or the impromptu acrobatics.

He's holding me in his arms like I'm light as a feather and makes no move to put me down. Maybe if I stay still and dream, I could find myself pressed up against Rick forever.

"Nice catch, Rickster." Ginger's snotty voice comes from somewhere. "You waiting for a trophy presentation? Put her down."

Reluctantly, I look away from Rick's chiseled face. I see that Ginger is calmly leaning on her machine, workout towel in hand. Her eyes are narrow and suspicious and glaring at Rick.

"Ginger," he nods. "How are you?"

Rick and Ginger regard each other with a shivery polite coolness and lock themselves into a stare-down. I can feel Rick's stomach muscles tense.

Rick Avery has a very hot, sexy, manly stomach.

My best friend and my secret gym crush have a history. I'm not aware of all the gory details because Ginger won't fully share them. From what I've pieced together, Rick's brother, Josh, and Ginger dated for a while a long time back, during high school.

It didn't end well, it seems. Younger brother Rick inadvertently interrupted some kind of impromptu interlude taking place in Josh's bedroom when Josh and Ginger were supposed to be studying. Enter younger brother Rick who wanted to see if someone wanted to play catch in the backyard.

Here's the kicker. Rick's parents heard Ginger's shrieking and ultimately discovered two mostly-disheveled teens up to some spicy activities that were not parent-approved.

There were groundings. Not to mention an embarrassing call to Ginger's parents.

Ultimately, the relationship fizzled.

"I think Harper hit you in the face?" Ginger is speaking to my He-man rescuer with a mocking lilt in her tone as she points to his head. "That's too bad."

I tilt my head upwards to inspect my hero closer. Have I, indeed, wounded my rescuer? Why, yes, I have. He has a big red splotch on his forehead and temple.

"Harper didn't do this." Rick looks back at my face with soft eyes as he answers. "Got kicked in the head by my sparring partner. Thought I'd take a break and grab a drink at the fountain." He tilts his head at the drinking unit attached to the wall behind the elliptical machines. "That's when I heard you ladies talking. Thought I'd say 'hi' and wish you a Merry Christmas."

Rick turns his attention back to me.

Ginger huffs.

"Thanks for saving Harper." Ginger half spits out the words and doesn't really sound overly grateful. "You can put her down now. I'll take care of her from here."

I'm not sure if Rick notices the insincerity or not. He complies, however, slowly sliding me down so my feet touch the floor and I'm into a pseudo standing position. Still, he keeps his hands at my waist and my posture tilted so I continue to lean into his torso.

He pulls his shoulders up in a little shrug. "Setting her up with Charlie isn't taking good care of her, Ginger."

"Eavesdropping, Rickster? Nice." Ginger scoffs slightly, but now her lips are curving slightly upwards. "Any chance I could ask your partner to kick you once more in the head? Perhaps you'll learn some manners."

Rick turns his head and locks his eyes with mine. "Harper Palmquist, you have a problem and I'm going to help. Would you do me the honor of being my Christmas Eve date next week?"

I blink. I don't look away from Rick's beautiful eyes. Not even when my hand comes up and rubs my forehead.

I thought I was dreaming. Then, I thought I wasn't. But now I'm assuming I'm back in the middle of a mirage.

I mumble to myself. "Funny. This all sort of seems like I'm conscious."

Ginger's voice hitches up an octave, and her attention clearly shows she is addressing Rick. "What are you doing?"

Rick breaks eye contact with me and seemingly looks up to address Ginger.

"Maybe something I've wanted to do for a long time."

"What?"

"I've thought about asking out Harper a bunch of times before, but she seemed to date a lot of guys. She never went out with them more than twice. Now I know why. You were setting her up with rejects. I'm rescuing her. For the second time today."

* * *

Rick Avery is back to gazing at me. Rick has asked me out on a date. A real date.

Of course, there's a problem.

My best friend and witness to the whole exchange is morbidly horrified at the concept.

Ginger's voice has taken on a shrill quality. "Ha-ha, Rick. Very funny. Please let my friend go. Now."

With seemingly great reluctance, Rick pushes me upright and gradually releases his grip on my torso. I'm standing straight for a couple of heartbeats, then start to tilt over again. My legs hurt.

In response to my 'Leaning Tower of Pisa' trick, Ginger and Rick each grab one of my arms and pull me away from the elliptical machines -- over to a group of chairs by the corner window. Each of them is on one side, and it's like I'm the rope in a human tug-of-war challenge.

Now in the corner, we now have some additional privacy.

My sparring duo of helpers are seated on either side of me and resume their verbal combat.

"Harper will not go out on a date with you, Rick."

I watch Ginger say this through clenched teeth. She's trying not to clench her teeth. But she's doing a bad job of no-clenching. She's not as pretty when her mouth is twisted up into a snarl.

Rick, for his part, seems unruffled. "How about you let your friend answer for herself? We're not in high school anymore where everyone does what you say all the time, Gin."

"Fine." Ginger huffs and she lets go of my arm. She crosses her own arms in front her chest, regarding Rick with obvious disdain. "Fine. I'm guessing Harper is more than capable of sniffing out a bad date risk when she sees one. Go ahead. Ask her again."

Rick looks over to my face. He opens his mouth, but then sort of freezes. No words come out. It's almost as if…he's nervous.

He moistens his lip. "Harper. I think you seem like a really nice person and I'd be honored if you'd spend Christmas Eve with me."

I soak the words in.

Rick Avery has a very hot, sexy, manly voice.

There's a long moment of silence. Finally, I speak.

"Am I imagining all this? You're asking me out on a first date? On Christmas Eve?"

Rick shifts uncomfortably. "Uh. Yeah."

"Why?"

Ginger emits a huff of satisfaction. "There you go, Rick. She's not as stupid as your usual chickadees. She has a brain and can see right through you."

Rick shifts in his seat. "Well, you seem very nice, Harper. Like someone that sort of might be…special."

"Special?"

"Special. In a really nice way."

"But, you're sort of the gym hottie…and I'm…sort of…not."

"Harper, you look like you have some sizzle to me." Rick grins.

Ginger clears her throat and mutters an "oh, brother" half under her breath, but loud enough for Rick and me to hear well enough.

Rick breaks his gaze with me to face Ginger. "Sucks for you, then, doesn't it? Seems the lady is considering my offer."

"She's being nice, you idiot." Ginger squints her eyes. "Go ahead. Seal the deal, Loverboy. You'll crash and burn all on your own with no help from me, either way. Give her one good reason why she should give you the time of day?"

My would-be suitor looks at me and shrugs. "Okay. Ready?"

I nod once. "Um…ready."

"I've wanted to ask you out for a long time, Harper." Rick grins a sexy grin. "But your best friend doesn't like me all that much. Besides, I sort of got the impression you were in a 'playing-the-field' kind of phase." He looks over at Ginger. "Didn't know that was just Gin playing flunkie matchmaker with her best friend."

Ginger gasps.

I gulp. Then, I blink. "Why doesn't Ginger like you?"

This is a ridiculous situation, really. Rick and I are talking about Ginger like she's not here when she's listening to our every word.

Rick takes in a deep breath and half-laughs a nervous exhale of the air. "Accidentally saw her once without her bra and she's embarrassed. Also, my brother kind of acted like an immature ass when they broke up." He shrugs one shoulder. "So I guess I thought you'd probably say 'no' even if I did make a move. Guys don't really like to be shut down. But now, I've got the chance to step up and see for sure what would happen and quit wondering. Merry Christmas to me."

"Oh." I look over my shoulder at Ginger, who continues to scowl. 'That's a...a pretty good answer."

Rick straightens his posture. "I overheard Gin talking about setting you up with Charlie. I know Charlie and he's not for you."

I lift one of my shoulders. "Is Charlie a bad guy?"

Rick visibly stiffens. He puts one hand on his hip and shakes his head. "No. Actually, Charlie is a really great guy. But very rigid. Too rigid for you, I think. How about the two of us go out instead? If it doesn't work, you could still go out with Charlie, later, right?"

Ginger has tightened her arms in front of her chest. She's also shaking her head. She doesn't want me to say 'yes.' But I think I'm going to take a chance on Rick Avery.

"Are you a bad guy?"

Rick bends both his legs at the knees uneasily. "Ah No. I think I'm a nice enough guy. Maybe a little rough around the edges because of my line of work, though."

I like this answer.

The truth is, I like guys that are a little rough around the edges. And I've had this little pitter-patter in my stomach for the last three months every time I've seen Rick Avery here.

I look over at Ginger. She is pursing her lips.

I bite my lower lip and look hopefully up at Rick. "I have an ongoing struggle with certain physical coordination tasks. Could we avoid dancing?" I decide to go for full disclosure before this discussion goes any further. "And bowling. Bowling and I are *not* good together."

Rick's facial features slowly evolve into a full-on smile. His gray-blue eyes pick up some sparkle and his mouth twists into a full-on grin. "Got it, bowling is out. Dancing is out."

Ginger clears her throat and we both turn her direction. She is watching Rick carefully, animosity gurgling from her entire body. "If you don't mind, Rick, where do you propose to take the woman who's the closest thing to a sister I'll ever have during your hypothetical date?"

Good question. I look back at Rick and await his.

His answer is a full-blown surprise and I feel my mouth fall open. "How would you feel about going to church?"

* * *

Rick Avery is a very manly, yet highly unpredictable man.

My hand is pressing at the base of my throat in horror. Someone as klutzy as me should not be around children for a long period of time.

Ever.

Ever ever.

And, Holy Father Christmas. Klutzy people like me certainly should *not* be in charge of children at a church. Especially during the course of *a first date*.

Though it might seem impossible to add a third layer of graduating awfulness, I have managed to do so. Seemingly without any effort whatsoever.

Think it through with me, will you? When everything goes awry on this first date in front of Rick…there are child witnesses everywhere. I can't even swear naughty words out loud.

Because I'll be in front of children.

And in a church.

First date. Children present. Children I'm in charge of helping to care for. No swearing.

It's my personal trifecta of doom.

The reality of my circumstances and their potential outcome hits me hard. This could be the worst date in the history of horrendous dates. In *anyone's* history.

I look to my side and my gaze catches on Rick for a long moment. He looks so handsome in his sport jacket and dress slacks. He's not wearing a tie. But the unbuttoned dress shirt looks positively scrumptious on him.

Rick Avery has very hot, sexy, manly attire.

He's watching me intently and gives me an occasional slight smile of encouragement. It's almost as if he can read my hysteria as clearly as if he is reading a newspaper. He winks at me and gives me a grin that clearly says *everything will be okay*.

Although hot and sexy -- Rick Avery may possess delusional tendencies.

"Harper, I'd like you to meet the Angel Chimes." Rick's smile deepens and the effect turns me warm in my red wrap holiday dress. My toes curl inside my pointy red shoes.

"Angel Chimes." I repeat the two words even as my voice cracks.

"The parents of these tots are in the adult bell choir. That's the group performing during the services at 1:00 p.m. and 3:00 p.m. These tykes play little bells at the beginning and end of two of the services. We're in charge of their supervision during their rest periods for the next two hours."

"Translation…we're the babysitters while their parents are busy."

Rick briefly rubs the miniscule stubble forming on his chin. "Yep. Pretty much."

"How did you…" I try to finish my question, but my voice fades from the terror welling up in my stomach.

"A friend recommended me for this volunteer gig." He pretends to have swagger, but he's actually teasing. I grin despite my nerves. "Besides that, I passed the background check with flying colors."

"Oh?"

"And the kids really seem to like me." Rick shrugs. "The boys know I'm a real-life bodyguard." My date stops to suggestively wiggle his eyebrows at me. "That gives me real-life, action figure coolness. The little girls like that I take turns from the boys and play Barbie dolls with them."

"You…play Barbies with the little girls?" My eyelashes flutter on their own accord, independently shocked.

"I do. Equal time for boys and girls. Race cars and dolls. Gotta be fair, don't I?" Rick winks at me again and gently puts a large, strong hand at the base of my spine.

Rick Avery has very hot, sexy, manly hands.

He leans in and his warm breath is soft, gently caressing my ear. "Have I told you how pretty you look this afternoon?"

I glance down at my red frock. "Um. Yes. Thanks." I look at all the children running about the room everywhere. "But I…should I…"

Rick reaches down to take my hand in his. "You're shaking." He chuckles. "You're not scared of kids, are you?"

I gulp. "Um." My teeth gently press down on my bottom lip. "Honestly? I'm guessing it's only a matter of time before I break them all." I scan the room and try to do a general guess on the head count. "Before I break…all twenty-five of them. And they cry. Loudly. At me." I spy the cases by the door that are full of little gold bells with black handles. "They'll cry right before they beat me with those…instruments out of revenge."

Thinking I am joking, Rick's laugh is spontaneous and loud and long. "I'll protect you from the hostile jingle bells."

Rick Avery has very hot, sexy laugh.

The sound of Rich laughing is truly beautiful and, suddenly, like puppies who hear the rustling of the treat bag -- all the kids stop what they are doing and take notice of the two of us by the door.

Little eyes lock on Rick. A moment later, fifty tiny feet in fancy dress shoes are stampeding to attack him from every direction.

"Mr. Rick!"

"'Very!"

"You're here!"

"Yay!"

None of the little munchkins notice me – which is great. My date's presence captures everyone's attention.

It takes me only a moment to figure out that some kids call Rick "Very" because "Mr. Avery" is too complicated to say easily. There are heated and near-incoherent requests by both the girls and boy children for Rick to join them in blocks, Barbies and some kind of race-car Transformer game first.

"We'll take turns. Just like usual." Rick calmly but firmly tells the ankle biters. Many of them are still wearing special white angel robes. "And my friend, Harper, needs to play with us, too."

The children freeze and slowly turn to give my presence their full attention. Their eyebrows wrinkle as they openly survey me.

One of the boys sniffs the air between him and Rick. He is wearing a bright red shirt underneath his white robe and, even at this young age, seems to carry himself with authority. "You smell funny, Very." He levels a frown at Rick.

One of his little peers holding a trio of racecars nods. He puts down his cars, then stands fully upright, wrinkling his nose in obvious disapproval. "My brother stinks like that when his goes to see his girlfriend. It's called 'calazone.' And I think people only wear it when they want to kiss other people."

The second little interrogator is giving me a serious look-over. I gulp.

A little girl corrects her friend's word choice. "It's 'cologne,' Davy." She regards me carefully. "And Very probably already kissed her."

I gulp again. I blush. I've not kissed Rick yet. I was hoping to kiss him later.

Rick Avery is probably a very hot, sexy kisser.

Suddenly all the children in the room swarm around us. We are the center in a huddle of little people.

Mr. Red Shirt continues his questioning as he folds his arms across his little chest. "Is she your girlfriend, Mr. Avery? Be honest."

Rick glances briefly at me, smiles sheepishly, then leans down on his haunches to make pseudo eye contact with the children who are only slightly taller than his knees.

He answers the question with a sort of stage whisper. "I'm trying to *make* her my girlfriend, guys, but you're sort of embarrassing me. Help me out here, dude."

A little girl with a frilly dress and bright nametag reading 'Allison' steps in, clearly wanting to come to the rescue in this dire situation. She glares at her male classmates. With a swishy skirt in motion, she hurries in front of the group, hands Rick a book and then loudly asks him her question.

"Will you read us this story?" She turns to me and smiles widely. She is missing a front baby tooth. "Mr. Rick knows how to read big words. You'll be 'mpressed."

Allison turns to the horde of rosy-cheeked mini-mob standing behind her. "Like that. You hafta help him 'mpress the lady by telling what Mr. Rick does fancy!"

One of Allison's friends hurries to my side to help her fearless leader-girlfriend.

"Do we need to move any of the tables around? Mr. Rick is strong and can do it EASY." She shakes her head up and down with emphasis. Then she lifts her arms at the elbows and flexes her nonexistent biceps at me for good measure. "Muscles! He doesn't even say naughty words when he moves big stuff like my g'anpa does, neither."

Clearly, I am supposed to be impressed. I make my eyes widen to imply the munchkin's efforts are working.

Mr. Red Shirt sees what he perceives to be a peer success and rushes to offer his own assurances next. "And he always says 'scuse me' when he toots!"

Another child rushes up behind me. "Mr. Rick always washes his hands after he blows his nose, too. And this one time, he helped the teacher change some poopy pan--"

"Okay, guys!" Rick claps his hands, interrupting his well-intending image consultants with a louder than necessary voice. "Thanks *so, SO much*, guys. How about we settle down and I'll read you this book, okay?"

I smile when I notice my date's cheeks. His face is flushed a manly shade of magenta.

Rick Avery is really handsome. Even when his face is red and he's embarrassed.

"Shouldn't read that one. It's about Rudolph!" One of the children points at the hardcover selection Rick has secured in his big, strong hands.

Allison, however, does not like having her reading selections questioned. "Rudolph has a girlfriend! This one is *romantic*!"

Worry burned onto his little features, the boy clarifies his concern. "But the girl reindeer might not like Rudolph because of his funny nose!" He points at Rick's face. "What if this lady looks at Mr. Rick's nose and 'cides she doesn't like it!"

Allison turns back to me, clearly opting to nip this concern in the bud. "Do you think Mr. Rick has a yucky nose?"

My jaw drops slightly open and I turn back to look at Rick. He is standing a few feet away from me, grinning. Oddly, except for a little blushing on his cheeks, he doesn't seem to be overly nervous.

I assume Rick is going to help me out and interrupt this interrogation. But he doesn't. He is silent. And then it becomes obvious he is waiting for my answer.

"Well...uh...no. I mean...Mr. Avery has a fine nose."

Rick Avery, indeed, has very nice, manly nose.

Another little girl swarms up from behind me and hugs my leg. "Mr. Rick almost broke his nose once when he got punched by a bad guy." She nods. "My mommy says Mr. Rick has a nice tushy."

Rick claps his hands together again. His face is deeper crimson now. "Hey, guys, tell you what. You go color me a bunch of Christmas pictures I can take home, and I'll bring juice boxes and raisins and fish crackers next week. Maybe even some cupcakes with frosting."

There's a rousing 'Yeah!' and other celebratory cheers before the two dozen or so ankle biters stampede off to the other end of the room.

Rick surveys the space around me to make sure all the children are out of earshot before he speaks again. His voice is a hushed whisper. The two sentences are clearly meant for my ears only.

"Glad to know word on the street is that I might have a nice tushy. You should check it out as I walk over there and help them find the crayons."

With that, he turns on the heels of his fancy shoes and walks towards where the children are settling into miniature chairs at miniature tables.

Instinctively, my eyes do fly to check out Rick's butt. I've done this before, of course, at the health club. But this time, I let my gaze linger for longer than ever before. After all, this is the only time I've been *invited* to look at my crush's derriere.

I know my conclusion long before I finish my inspection, of course. Allison's mom is right.

Rick Avery has an exceptionally stellar tushy.

* * *

I consult my watch.

Twenty more minutes and I'm home free or *olly olly oxen free* or whatever the heck the phrase is.

And notice, I said 'heck' successfully and didn't substitute a naughtier word that would not be appropriate for usage whilst one is in a church.

Only twenty more minutes until Rich and I will complete our shift watching these adorable, yet exhausting, children and the parents will begin to pick them up.

We've actually had a very nice date, under the circumstances.

My date has, to the delight of his youthful audience, colored me a picture of a snowman.

Later, we had some enormous fun shooting foam balls at one another with slingshots during a David and Goliath contest.

And not to be overlooked, he shared his fish cracker snacks with me when we were a package short.

We've laughed. We've hurled fake biblical rocks. We've shared crackers. The sense of a potential successful date is making butterflies do a dance in my stomach.

One of my new little girlfriend buddies has even insisted I carry around a dress-up purse full of jingle bells. The cross-body-like mini-messenger bag slings over my shoulder and hip like a second skin. Soft chimes ring out when I bump the satchel just right. I wear the bag proudly, like a trophy of acceptance. I hope the kids think I am worthy of being Rick's girlfriend. I mean, I'm sure they don't award this coveted assortment of music-makers to just *anyone*, you know?

What was I worried about, anyway? Really. I've been crazy worrying I wasn't good enough to even be in the same league as the workout gym hottie.

Funny thing. We've had a great time.

He likes me. He has to. He's even teased me into checking out his butt.

Hmmm. What if he wasn't actually teasing?

I shrug to myself. Oh, who cares if he was teasing or not! I am on a date…a real-life date with a guy I like. And, I think, likes me. Plus, it's Christmas Eve. And nothing horrible has happened! Maybe my holidays aren't cursed after all.

Bliss washes over me in waves as I watch Rick and the other two teachers on duty play and read with children in various corners of the room. I smile as I pick up a few of the jingle bell bracelet toys that didn't make it into the shoulder bag storage.

It's then that I hear the sound. *Thud, thud. Thud, thud.* I turn behind me and realize it's someone knocking on the room door. The large wooden block features a tiny window in the center, like a super-sized peephole.

With curious frown, I peek through the window. A young woman with staticky red hair is waving at me and showing me her little badge that reads 'Church Security" on the tab.

I turn the knob and open the door slowly. Miss Red Hair pushes the door open with a harder jolt. She's wearing the tan pants and black shirts that I see many employees wearing tonight. She even has the requisite mistletoe flower pinned on her collar, just as I do, signaling to everyone that she's some sort of official employee.

"Hi. I'm Valerie and I need to pick up Cayden and bring him to his mom downstairs."

Her eyes don't meet mine as she quickly scans the room and locates the little boy in the green sweater and tan pants. She waves at him and Cayden immediately runs over to greet the woman.

"Hi, Aun—shumeunshen." Cayden has started to talk to the security woman, but Red immediately smushes Cayden's mouth, and the affectionate gesture drowns out the little boy's words.

"Hi Cayden! You need to come with me, 'kay? We're going to meet your mom."

Without waiting for a reply, the woman scoops up the little boy and presents a Tootsie Roll, already half-unwrapped.

With a "thanks" at me over her shoulder, she turns to leave the room, walking quickly.

The hairs on the back of my neck prickle. Something doesn't feel right.

I start to go over and ask a nearby child reading a book about finding the signout sheet I've heard about. It's only then that I see the wooden hook with the name "Cayden" glued on in un-straight puffy letters at the coat area.

Cayden's little coat still hangs there, waiting patiently on the curved knob.

The details flip through my head as if I am doing those addition cards in elementary school. Something isn't adding up.

I have a mom. I've watched countless television sitcoms with moms.

Moms provide constant reminders about coats on cold days. Moms instruct approved caregivers to pick up children and their coats. In fact, they nag people. About vegetables and brushing their teeth…*and coats.*

In fact, moms nag children to put on their coats and nag loads of other people entrusted to their care to not forget collecting coats when they are collecting their precious children.

It occurs to me that Cayden was still wearing his white robe, too. Any legitimate caregiver would have been reminded to make sure he takes off his white robe, surely.

In a full panic, I know there aren't even a handful of seconds to spare.

I rush over to my date. I don't have time to explain all this. Besides, what if Rick doesn't believe me? What if he thinks I'm being silly when I know – *I know* – something isn't right with Cayden's pick-up person?

I have to act fast. It's vital I swoop into action…but its likely best to avoid a kid panic by announcing to my charges that I've let one of their peers become preschooler-napped.

An idea that can save time pops into my mind.

Of course, if this works, Rick will probably be mad. But I don't have time to come up with a "Plan B," so I lurch forward.

"Hey, uh, Rick." My voice is a little shrill. I hurry across the room, interrupting him as he reads a story.

"Harper, could I finish this—"

"No!" I push enthusiasm from my voice. "I want to play…*play police*. Right now! You have to be fair. I need a turn! I need a turn!"

"Well –"

"What does this do?" I point to the black rectangle with the antennae hanging on his belt.

The frown on Rick's forehead deepens. He's sensing something isn't quite right.

"Show all of us how your walkie-talkie security thing works, okay? Can I hold it? I'll be the police person! How do I turn it on?"

My questions erupt from my mouth with alarming speed and practically merge together. I wiggle my fingers in the air to try and show my enthusiasm for touching forbidden electronics gear.

Rick hand reaches down at the black electronic unit clipped to his belt. His fingers are unsure and unsteady. "You want to see my security radio?"

He unhooks it and I see the big red button with "ALERT" embossed in raised letters.

"My turn!" I grab the unit and turn to all the little kids watching me with rapt attention. "Let's play kidnapper!"

"Kidnap--?" Rick doesn't even get the full word out before I launch into my plan.

I push the red button three times for good measure while I make a run for the door.

"Mayday, Mayday! This is Harper and I'm a…I'm a Preschool Teacher Helper and a boy in a white dress has been stolen."

I turn to all the children, watching me with rapt attention. I stage whisper to them. "Go hide under the tables, okay! Like…like one of those tornado drills! Isn't this fun?"

The children scamper away at warp speed. They listen and obey with alarming efficiency.

There is static on the radio. There's no way to gauge if anyone is listening there.

"I repeat. A woman kidnapper with a boy wearing a white dress – I mean, white gown. The boy is in the dress. Not the woman. The woman is the kidnapper!"

Rick is trying to approach me, confusion wrinkled up in his eyebrows. But a half-dozen kids are glomming onto his legs and trying to push him under a little table – essentially rendering him useless for my upcoming hot pursuit needs.

I turn and half run out of the room, then break into a full run once I reach the hallway.

I don't know if anyone is listening or not. I hope so! I remember a cop television show I saw once and try to remember how the people talked into their little handheld boxes with the curly black cord.

It would take me too long to unpeel children from my date. It is the best course of action if I continue to take matters into my own hands.

I hurry from the room as fast as my fancy red shoes will take me.

A moment later, I'm running down the hall and reach the stairway balcony. I scan the stairs in every direction. Miraculously, I see my church volunteer imposter on the last flight of stairs. Cayden is obviously pulling back now, pushing away from his captor. His arm is rigid and long and his feet are pushing back against the short carpeting.

I call out to the woman to wait. Instead of stopping, she picks up the pace and hurries away from me.

I need help and glance around me. No one.

With a determined scowl, I survey my radio. I push the red button again.

"The boy's name is Cayden. The woman has a badge, but she doesn't have his coat. She had candy and she's got to be a liar because she didn't take the boy out of the white dress. There are hangars for the dresses!"

"Is this for real?" Someone inside the radio asks, pointedly.

Before I can answer, another security radio voice talks back to me. "Roger, that. Preschool helper. Team, follow standard protocol." There's a brief shhhshhh sound of static and then words that are music to my ears. "Seal the exits. I repeat. Seal the chapel exits."

I hurry down the stairs and see the woman and Cayden. They're walking by the big tree with the blinking lights. She stops, noticing all the other people in black t-shirts moving towards the heavy glass doors. She turns around and starts heading in another direction. It's the handicap ramp exit. No security people are in place there.

If she makes it to the door, she can go up to the balcony or out the doors to the parking lot. Neither destination strikes me as particularly safe.

I see the side access stairs. I kick off my impractical high-heeled shoes and run to intercept my targets. Cayden's shrill yelling can now be heard just above the cocktail party-like crowd murmur.

With a backward glance, I see Rick coming down the hallway behind me. He has to pause to locate me in the crowd. He breaks into a run as he glances up from his hand. It looks like he has acquired another security radio.

I could wait for him. But, I don't. Cayden needs me.

I hurry down the second set of stairs faster and break into a full-blown sprint.

Up ahead, I see that the female kidnapper is nearly at the entrance doors. She sees me and I can see the fear on her face. Her eyes have widened and her mouth is circling into an "O" shape.

Seconds later, we are only a few feet from each other. She stops abruptly and reaches for something in her back pocket.

Then, it happens. Just like in the gym. My surroundings suddenly start to blur as I feel myself moving as if in slow motion.

I will have a security confrontation here. In a church, surrounded by Christmas trees and lights. By a donut bar. On a first date with a hot guy. Nothing odd here, I tell myself. I'm sure this sort of thing happens all the time.

My target's back pocket bulges with something sinister. Like mace. Or worse.

It's time for me to prepare for the presentation of something ominous. I have no weapon or shield.

A soft chiming sound distracts me…and I look down. My elbow has accidentally bumped into the bag over my shoulder.

My eyes survey this possession with new awareness. The jingle bell bag. A bag full of jingle bells. Maybe the little orbs of metal aren't *exactly* bullets.

But they're pretty close when you think about it. Round, tuneful pellets.

Jingle bell *bullets*.

My newspaper obituary could potentially reference I went down in a blaze of…well, bells. But that's okay. I fought…fought with every resource available to me. There's got to be some dignity in that.

Musical projectiles are nothing to discount. It's been approximately an hour since a little boy pelted one at a friend when there was a shortage of crackers. I've seen first-hand the savage carnage – well, crying -- a single bell can dispense. And I have more than one, even. As the rough-and-tumble cop would mutter to his sidekick in an action movie…*I am locked and loaded.*

I drop the security radio to the floor, immediately dig into the bag and begin hurling wave after wave of jingle bells at the kidnapper. Wave one hits my target's chest. The second assault hits the floor just in front of kidnapper woman. The third handful hits her knees.

Her grip on Cayden loosens and the kidnapper slides him to the floor gently with one arm. Little silver balls tinkle in stereo as they roll on the floor. She steps away, but her shoes step on the orbs of metal.

And then, just as in the television cartoons, my would-be kidnapper's feet fly into the air as a look of surprise washes over her face. The woman's eyebrows fly up into her forehead. Her hands fly up in alarm as she tries to regain her balance.

There's a loud thumping sound as she hits the floor, landing on her back.

Bells are still ringing as Rick appears next to me. He's been running…and then he stops. While Ms. Kidnapper lays there groaning, Cayden pushes up, starts crying and runs. He runs away from the kidnapper…runs past me…and launches himself at Rick's leg, clutching his knees.

Rick calls out to one of the security officials. He's alerted parking guards to swarm the outside door and call the police. My date, essentially, has been arranging for backup in case no one was listening to my radio alerts. When you think about it, that's sort of sweet.

As the kidnapper rolls to her side, I see something unexpected in her hand.

It's not a knife of a gun or a taser. Confused, I try to identify the item.

Funny. It looks like a brochure.

* * *

Ginger is on the elliptical machine next to me. This is the first time ever my exercise pace is overwhelmingly faster than hers. Thanks to embarrassment –induced adrenaline, my pace is impressive.

Comparatively, Ginger's pacing is drastically reduced because she's laughing so hard. Her face is red and one of her hands is pushing at her stomach as she tries to control her extended outburst.

"So…" Ginger sputters, her lips quivering from amusement. "I'm sorry to ask you to tell this story again, but I want to get it straight. The kidnapper is the boy's aunt?"

My teeth grind against one another slightly. "Yes."

My voice is purposefully tight and my words clipped. I am explaining this for the fourth time. My face is red. Red with embarrassment. But I'm hoping that to any innocent bystander, my face looks red due to physical exertion.

Ginger begins to laugh harder. Eventually, she regains control.

"The aunt was mad the sister didn't appreciate the expensive GPS location belt buckle she bought the boy as a Christmas gift."

Ginger emits more sputter laughing.

"And the police eventually read the brochure and talk to everyone. And then everyone goes home for Christmas dinner. After being chased by the police in the middle of a church service?"

"Yes." I grit my teeth.

"A chase that you led *everyone* in. You, who stole a walkie-talkie from a potential would-be boyfriend."

I struggle to keep my voice semi-patient. "Like I said. The mom wanted the aunt to buy Cayden a train set. But she bought the belt buckle with the GPS chip instead. There was an argument. An argument that inspired the aunt to try and script an event that showed she's right."

Ginger is now laughing so hard she has to stop exercising. She steps off her machine. "So the aunt wants to prove a point. Without parental permission, she breaks the nephew out of Church Angel Chime childcare."

"Yes."

"And, then, she plans to hide out with him in the balcony until mom finds her son gone and reluctantly calls in to activate the belt buckle service. And then the aunt is a hero and has given her nephew the best Christmas present in the world." Ginger wipes at the tears in her eyes. "Ohmygoodness."

"Kidnapping is not funny, Gin."

"But the plan goes awry when you go all "Charlie's Angels" in the preschool ward and thwart an aunt's diabolical

plan!" Ginger is near hysterical, now. Her crying hitches up a
notch. "You arm yourself with a bad bag of jingle bells, a walkie
talkie you don't know how to use and take off in…in *hot
pursuit*…in red sparkly shoes!"

I bristle as Ginger loses her composure once more from a
fit of all-consuming laughter.

"Like I said, no one is pressing any charges. On anyone.
The sisters both apologized to each other. The church officials
made both women promise to do some volunteering as restitution.
It was all over before the choir sang *Silent Night*, okay? Amen.
And let's not talk about it anymore."

Ginger's laughter quiets even as her chest is heaving. She
is, apparently, struggling to make any of her limbs work in concert
with the others. Her face is red and tears are streaming down her
cheeks. She pushes a workout towel casually to her face – to blot
the tears, not to address her non-existent workout sweat.

"We have to talk about it some more. Because here is my
favorite part."

"Gin, please."

"So after the sisters and you give your police statements,
you are released." Her face turns somewhat serious for a brief
moment. "That's when you decide you are too mortified to face
Rick, right?"

I huff a soft puff of air out of my lungs. "Can't we just say
I was suddenly inspired to join the choir?"

"You were inspired to join the choir so you could avoid facing Rick, you mean."

I toss my hands in the air. "My date with the hottest guy on the planet has evolved into an event that's the current laughingstock of the local police department. Really? Can you blame me for trying not to amp up the punch line any higher? I just put on a choir gown and blended in with the choir. Eventually, I even learned some of the songs. I brought the joy of song to--"

"Save it, choir recruit," Ginger folds her arm and frowns at me. "So you admit you ditched him?"

I roll my eyes in exasperation. "Hasn't the poor man been through enough already? So what if I camouflage myself as a member of the church choir for two hours."

"So you admit you're a coward? It's insult to injury. You ditch him after you steal his police CB-thing."

"It's a *security radio*, if you must know. And I just *acquired* the radio…sort of under false pretenses. But that's not the point."

"Sounds a little like fraud. Or stealing. And either way, it's not healthy. You need closure. Face hottie pants like a man. Not like a little girl who pretends to join the choir for a day."

"No, thanks." I push my feet to make the elliptical machine go faster. "Look. We don't need to go over all the gory details. The highlight reel is simple. I had a first date that went awry. I am now well-churched. And it's imperative we meet here at random workout times I approve."

"Because you intend to fully avoid seeing Rick ever again."

"Yes."

Ginger wipes the last of the tears from her face with the back of her hand. "You should call him back. Really. It's been a full 48-hours since his date took a bite out of crime in his church lobby." Ginger chuckles at her clever entendre. "The man just wants to talk to you and you, frankly, owe him at least that. Besides, if he talks to you, he'll finally stop calling me and I can recover from the horrid flight home."

I glare at my best friend. "Since when do *you* care about being fair to Rick Avery? Newsflash reminder, here. You *hate* Rick. I would have thought you'd be happy I'm trying to avoid him and let the memory of our disaster date become a great ghost story of Christmas past."

Ginger shrugs. But I note the growing devious smile on her face. The nonverbal cue of her mood matches the naughty glimmer in her eyes.

"He likes you. You like him, too. He cares about you. In a real way."

"I'm a walking dating disaster, Ginger. You want the summary. Fine. I like Rick too much to put him through the food processor that includes ingredient Harper."

"You're being ridiculous." My best friend pauses and glances over her shoulder. "You aren't poison." She pauses again.

"More like a very specific spice that has to be used in only very select recipes."

"Face it, Gin. I'm a danger to date. Not just for sane guys like Charlie. But even for guys fully-trained in weapons and combat."

Ginger nods. "Whatever. Here we go. You can thank me for this later." She reaches over to my control console and pushes the buttons to make it kick into warp speed.

"Huh?" My legs scramble to keep up, confused as to what my best friend is doing. I try to adjust my pacing.

Then Ginger suddenly punches the big red Stop button.

It's a déjà vu moment. Once again, I'm flying in the air, my favorite elliptical machine is, no doubt, laughing at me behind all the blinking lights on the console.

I fly. Backwards.

Strong arms catch me. Familiar strong arms…my shoulder and cheek press into a hard chest.

A familiar scent.

I look up to confirm what my pounding heart already knows to be true.

A tilt of my head reveals Rick Avery grinning down at me. Our eyes lock.

"Nice catch. Again." Ginger's voice comes from somewhere, but Rick and I don't break our gaze. "Heard enough, then?"

"Yeah. Heard enough. Thanks."

Rick is holding me in his arms.

Thanks?

"Call me later, Harper." Ginger's voice is fading, and only then, do I pull my focus to look for my friend. She's walking out of the room, not even giving me a backward glance of concern.

"You're...leaving me?" I call out the question to her backside.

The back of Ginger's hand waves at me. The square diamond on her ring finger winks at me once again. The sparkle is a happy glimmer, almost as if the gem is amused at my expense.

"Work out your issues with Rick, Harper. Call me later. After I've slept off the jet lag." Ginger pauses. "Rick, quit calling me. Do you have any idea how long the flight is from Hawaii? Let me sleep, already."

"This is...so *uncool*." My cranky voice calls out to Ginger.

To her credit, she stops briefly. She tosses me a long, backwards look. "Make no mistake, Harp. Rick is the one in trouble. Although fully aware of the 'danger' that likely goes with dating you, he's still interested. Poor guy." Ginger shakes her head solemnly, then continues walking around the corner.

Angry with my friend, I still have to face facts. Rick is holding me easily in his arms -- smiling at me like a Cheshire cat.

Blast him. He looks perfect...and smells delicious.

Meanwhile, I'm a sweaty and wilted ponytail mess of human elliptical machine cannonball.

"Look what I caught again, will you?" Rick's voice is a husky vibration that I feel in his chest as well as hear under my tousled exercise clothes. "How 'bout we clear the air a bit?"

I gulp.

Rick asks me a simple question, then. One I'm not expecting. "They have great cookies downstairs. Want to join me for one?"

* * *

It's a tense situation. Two oatmeal raisin cookies sit on little paper plates in front of us. Both remain untouched.

We are sitting at a small table in the very corner of the balcony that overlooks the tennis courts. Clear glass and strong wall secures us on three sides from fast, unexpected runaway balls. Despite all of the safety glass, I am a mess of anxiety.

Rick and I eye one another over the uneaten treats sitting on the table between us. This is my first cookie standoff – and I'm not sure what to expect.

After a long silence, I decide to go first.

"You got my friend to set me up." My breathing is lightly shallow, from earlier exercise and other recent unexpected surprises.

Rick nods once. "Guilty as charged."

I purse my mouth. "You were eavesdropping on our conversation. Probably hiding behind me or behind the water fountain wall."

Rick tips his head and provides a second affirmative acknowledgement. "Affirmative."

I moisten my bottom lip, readying myself to speak. My tongue feels the quivering and sends in my teeth to gently try and steady myself.

"You never have to see me again." I blurt this out quickly.

"I'd like for us to go out again." Rick's rich voice is a full octave lower than mine.

Both Rick and I have the serendipity to speak at the exact same time. Trouble is, we have totally different ideas on the nature of how our future together should go.

Rick appears to give either me or my cookie some serious consideration, as proven by the gentle squinting of his left eye.

Rick Avery is a very handsome guy, even when he squints.

"Mind if I ask why you don't want to go out with me again?"

Pretty women in short tennis skirts are walking nearby, all taking second looks at the fact that I, plain-Jane Harper, am sitting at a table with hottie-yum-a-lottie Rick Avery.

"For starters, I nearly caused unprecedented carnage to various people. On our first date. Which only lasted a few hours."

"Carnage?" Rick echoes my word choice as he raises an eyebrow. "Wow. Think you're pretty dangerous, don't you?"

"I know." I release a breath I didn't know I was holding. "Clearly, it's better if we don't see what I am capable of on a second date."

Rick winces. "Thought we had a little chemistry going."

I blink twice. "All the women who come here drool over you, even as we sit here. You could…could choose any of them."

"What if I choose you?"

I lower my eyebrows into what I hope is an adequately grave expression. For added measure, I shake my head. "Do you have a death wish?"

"No." Rick answers simply. "Although, I have been called an adrenaline junkie a couple of times."

I nearly choke on a gasp of air. "Yes, well. I think that explains a lot."

"All things considered, I didn't think our first date was that bad."

I push both my hands into the space atop the corners of our little square table to steady myself.

"Um. I *stole* your talkie thing, *attacked* a woman with jingle bells, quite probably *traumatized* a little boy and ultimately was *involved* in a misunderstanding which ultimately necessitated police involvement. That adds up to a disaster. On *any* date." I pause. "Unless this is your standard date – and in that case, a second date is out for completely different reason."

Rick grins, then shrugs. "Harper, you are absolutely not my standard date. Kind of a change of pace for me to date someone who cares so much about kids she barely knows that she practically full on tackles a potential perp."

"I got some facts wrong."

"Better safe than sorry. Especially in my business. Besides, doesn't mean you'll get 'em wrong next time."

"That's nice of you to say."

Rick lifts a shoulder and leans over the table, lowering his voice to a conspiratorial whisper. "Your best friend doesn't seem to hate me quite as much as she did last week. Give it another week or so, and who knows what could happen."

"Provided you survive."

Rick nods and pretends to give my comment serious thought. "Good thing I'm certified in advanced CPR and well-trained in a number of other survival techniques. I'll take my chances."

One of my shoulders tentatively reaches up to my ear. "That might not be enough."

Rick thoughtfully pokes his tongue into the inside of his cheek.

"Would it help if I freshen up on my bomb detonation training before we go out again?"

"Bomb detona...." I wince and my voice fades for a moment. "That the problem. You never know with me."

My companion chuckles.

Rick Avery has very hot, sexy, laugh.

The laugh settles into a grin. "Here's the deal, Harper. I like you. A lot." He pauses. "You're fun to talk to. And nice. And pretty. And I love watching your enthusiasm when you run down here and eat cookies after your workouts. And I just..."

I freeze.

"I just find myself wanting to talk to you," Rick clarifies. "Maybe I need to find out if kissing you would be as great in real life as I imagine it might be when I'm watching you lick cookie crumbs off your lips."

"You…you've been watching me eat cookies?"

"Harper, I've been watching you for forever. I've seen you open the door for the old man who plays racquetball here every Saturday morning and help unwind a lady's shoe from the pedals upstairs and be a really nice person." Rick shrugs then. "At first, I thought it was impossible for someone to be as nice and unpredictable as you. But I think you're exactly who I think you are and I'd like to get to know you better on a second date."

"Oh."

"Plus, it's cool to date a chick who can handle would-be criminals."

"Um…"

"Any chance, here that if I play my cards right, say all the right things here in the right order, you might consider going out with me on a second date?'

I half shrug. "You don't mind dating someone known to have some proficiency with musical weaponry?"

Rick grins. "Don't mind at all. Sorta exciting."

"Really?" I pause, and then I smile. "Well, be warned I might need you to sign a disclaimer so you don't sue me in the event there's another incident with bells."

"Darlin', you can be my jingle bell bodyguard anytime."

Rick's eyebrows wiggle suggestively. "Provided I can be yours."

Rick Avery has very sexy, manly eyebrows.

Home for Christmas

By

Susan Craig

Dear Reader:

April Windham's story, *Home for Christmas*, is about new beginnings in old surroundings. April hasn't had it easy. In my "*Toss*" trilogy, she was absent from *Tossing the Caber*, a bit player in *Toss Up*, then an antagonist in *Tossed and Tumbled*. Poor April had to leave York, PA and move to St. Louis during a freak snowstorm to get her own story. After you read it, I hope you'll agree it was worth the wait!

Check out my website www.susancraigromance.com for more info about the "*Toss*" trilogy and other things I write. Wishing you a wonderful holiday season…

Sincerely,

~ Susan

I

Snow whipped across the road, obscuring April's vision. The windshield wipers of her Hyundai pumped furiously, but didn't help. The broad expanse of concrete that was Interstate 70 was empty—at least she hoped it was empty. She couldn't see more than twenty feet in front of her, the lines on the road were obscured by a curtain of white, and the last glimpse she'd had of a sign—snow-covered and unreadable—had been at least half an hour ago.

"This is bad news," she moaned. "Why didn't I pull over when I had the chance?" She'd driven through several brief flurries, but with a CD in the player, she'd had no way of knowing they were just the ragged edge of the worst blizzard to hit western Illinois in fifty years. Besides, a woman alone, parked on the side of the road at two in the morning? That wasn't such a good idea either.

"There is a traveler's advisory for Interstate 70," intoned a brisk male voice. She'd turned the radio on when conditions worsened—too late, apparently. "Whiteout conditions are intermittent; the interstate has been closed from Altamont to Troy. Repeat, the interstate is closed from Altamont to Troy."

"Oh, shut up." April unclamped one hand from its death grip on the steering wheel and twisted the dial, turning off the radio. Was she in the closed part? She had no idea. If there'd been signs or warnings, she hadn't seen them. She didn't dare stop now, in the middle of the highway, and she was afraid to pull over because she couldn't see the shoulder of the road. There was nothing to do but keep driving. If the road was closed, there would be no help if she drove off the edge, or stopped and got stuck. At least there were no drifts. The wind powering the whiteout was blowing too hard to let the snow settle on the road for long.

What had ever possessed her to drive to St. Louis pulling a trailer? She should have hired movers, or shipped the antique bedroom suite, instead of trying to bring it along herself. But she felt better having it with her. It was all she had left of her mom's furniture—the one thing she hadn't been able to part with. And who would expect a snowstorm this early in October? As she squinted at the white-on-white swirls of snow illuminated by her headlights, she saw a tall narrow post pass to the left of her car. A road sign. She was headed off the edge of the road. Panicked, she slammed on the brakes and slid silently off the highway and down an incline.

Inside the car, April heard a scream as she fought to steer the car into the skid. It was her own. Going straight ahead down the incline was her only chance to avoid rolling both car and trailer. Time slowed to a crawl, every second stretched to the max, as her mind shifted into high gear, calculating with lightning speed the motions required to save her life. A small part of her brain planned what steps to take if the car drove onto ice over a lake, what to do if the ice broke, how to react if she ran into a tree or other obstruction. As her mind flew, the skid slowed, and car and trailer drifted to a stop—safe, but whether by inches or by a mile she had no idea.

April shuddered. She switched off the engine and her head dropped to the steering wheel as she fought to catch her breath.

It might have been one minute, or it might have been fifteen, when the cold creeping into the car caused her to raise her head again. There was nothing to see outside the window but snow. She pushed the key back into the ignition and started the engine. Her cell phone was on the car charger. Reaching for it, she saw that the green light on the charger was dark. *Oh no. I just bumped it coming down the hill, right?*

Wrong. The charger, which was a bit finicky, hadn't been twisted properly into the outlet. Her phone was dead. She reached to turn off the engine, conserve fuel, then stopped. She couldn't risk driving, but she had to stay warm, and the lights on the car were her only hope of being found before morning. Maybe running the engine would be enough to keep the battery charged and the lights working.

Grateful that she had put a box of bedding in the back seat of the car, she unbuckled her seatbelt and turned around to dig for a blanket. Make that two blankets. Flopping back down, she opened the first and draped it over her legs and chest, and then unfolded the second and wrapped it over her coat like a huge shawl. She refused to think about how fast the car would cool in the howling wind once the gasoline ran out. Pulling out the button for the hazard flashers—even if someone was on the road, would they see the lights with the trailer behind her?—she scooted to the center of the seat, away from the cold reaching through the metal and glass of the doors, and curled up with her eyes shut. The snow seemed less menacing when she couldn't see it.

Panic bubbled up inside her. Her mind sought refuge from the fear, and she began to speak, reciting words she had memorized at her mother's knee decades before. "The Lord is my shepherd, I shall not want…"

II

The car was nearly buried, with no sign of life around it. Max Moretti looked at the unmarked snow. If it hadn't been for the trailer, he'd never have spotted the car. And if it hadn't been for the speed limit sign bent at a 45-degree angle to the ground, he'd probably have missed the trailer as well.

Max signed heavily and turned up the collar of his sheepskin jacket. There was no avoiding it. He would have to go check the car. It was probably a fool's errand; the trailer was iced over and might have been there for days. The sun, rising low in a cloudless sky, glittered over the glacial landscape. It was bitter cold. Hell, even if he had hip boots he'd get soaked to the skin digging down to the car. It was little more than a snow-covered bump at the bottom of the shoulder.

Stop stalling, Moretti. Just do it. He swung the door of his truck open and stepped out.

Slipping and sliding down the slope, he cursed himself for being an idiot. *Should have just called and reported it. If I twist an ankle, I'll have to call 911 to come rescue me.*

But calling for help just wasn't Max's style. Sweeping his arm across the windshield to clear away the snow, he peered inside.

A body.

Adrenaline jolted through his veins.

A woman. She wasn't moving. He couldn't see well enough to tell more than that. Raking snow off the driver's-side window, he let more light into the interior and pounded on the windshield with his fist. "Hey, wake up! Wake up!"

He dug into the snow, found the door handle and pulled. Nothing. It was either locked or iced up. With a few strong swipes of his arms, he cleared the snow from the roof of the car and hammered on it with both fists. The racket he was making echoed in the crystal air. He ducked his head down to look in the window again. She had moved. He pounded on the roof again. Louder. Longer. A face turned toward him and he watched her try, clumsily, to open the door. On the third try, she managed to lift the handle. He heard the lock disengage and yanked the car door open. She was as white as the landscape, with hair that looked blood-red in the morning light. Pale lips trembled and huge gray eyes stared at him, uncomprehending.

"Get out. My truck—up there—it's warm. You're frozen."

When she didn't move, he simply reached in and grabbed her blanket-wrapped body, hauling her out into the daylight, setting her on her feet next to him. She sank into the snow.

"Whoa. Try again." He hauled her back up, but it was no good. Her legs wouldn't bear her weight.

Max slammed the door of the car, then bent and shoved a shoulder in the vicinity of her belly, draping her over his back in a fireman's carry. He turned and scrambled back up to the road, hanging onto her legs with an arm behind the knees and using his free hand to stabilize himself on what had to be the original slippery slope. Nearly on all fours, he reached the top and heaved himself upright. The cold seeped through his wet jeans and numbed his toes. Yanking open the passenger door of his truck, he shoved her inside and shut the door. Circling around to the driver's side, he clambered in beside her.

She still didn't speak, but her eyes were open. They followed his every move.

Turning the key in the ignition, he revved the engine. "We're going somewhere warm. Relax." Max kicked the heater up to full blast, shivering as the still-cool air pulled more heat from his damp thighs. Below the knees, his legs were too cold to notice the change.

Well, they would warm up soon. Now where to take the human icicle? Damn, her hair was glorious. Neither short nor long, and straight as silk, it fell in disarray about her face. But the color. He'd had a weakness for redheads since forever. Twelve years old he'd been, when a red-headed babysitter had ruined him for any hair color that didn't gleam like burnished copper in firelight. He smiled at the memory. She had starred in his adolescent fantasies for years.

The woman in the cab beside him had hair like that. *Probably from a bottle.* But that didn't stop the warmth inside from growing each time he glanced at her. *Okay, Moretti, enough with the hair. She's more than half frozen.* Where to take her? He hadn't driven this road in years, but they should be coming to civilization soon.

* * *

Finally. Max squinted through his dark glasses, trying to read the price on the motel sign against the glare of the sun. *Doesn't matter.* All the national chains charged about the same anyhow. He pulled up to the lobby and stopped.

"I'm getting a room here. You have to get warm and then we can worry about your car and trailer."

The woman nodded briefly, jaw tight.

Was she mute or what? No matter. He stepped from the truck, putting the ignition key in his pocket. After all, he knew nothing about her. Stepping to the door of the motel lobby, he swung it open and walked up to the desk. It was hours before check-in, but Max wasn't worried about that. He'd explain the situation—or pay a little extra—and they'd have a room and warmth in no time at all.

* * *

April didn't protest when the tall, dark man nudged her into the motel bathroom.

"Ladies first," he said, and shut the door behind her.

Her body shuddered from the bone-deep cold, but her mind burned with unanswered questions. Who was her rescuer? What were his intentions? She had no I.D., no money, no phone. She was in a motel room with a stranger. She stepped to the bathroom door and twisted the lock, then relaxed for the first time since she'd been jolted back to wakefulness that morning.

She hadn't expected to wake up ever again.

At first, she'd been convinced the noisy stranger was a final pre-death hallucination, and been annoyed. Other people got beckoned toward the light. Why was she stuck with some idiot pounding on the top of her car and dragging her into sunshine so bright it made her eyes water?

But when she fell into the snow, reality began to take hold. She was alive. This was real. And now… Now she could be in real trouble.

Maybe he was an angel… Her mind's eye saw the tight-set line of his whisker-roughened jaw, not yet a beard but too much to be called stubble. Clearly, he didn't care what people thought of his appearance. Her palm tingled, as she wondered what it would feel like to touch his face.

Stop that. He could be a psycho. And no way is he an angel.

Dark hair in half-curls, its length—like the whiskers—in the unkempt zone between well-groomed and deliberate statement. Strong brows, deep-set eyes, and a mouth turned down at the corners. The mouth eased her mind somewhat. He didn't look pleased with the situation. A dangerous nutcase would be pretending to be nice, wouldn't he? And jumping for joy inside…

She sat down and buried her head in her hands. *What am I going to do?*

She couldn't hide in the bathroom forever, and her cell phone was lying dead in her car with everything else she owned, somewhere in the snow along highway 70.

Do the next thing. That was the best piece of advice she'd gotten from the therapist she'd seen when her mom's battle with cancer had threatened to overwhelm them both. It had come in handy many times over the last four years.

All right. Warm up in a hot bath, stay alert, and pray that he truly is a Good Samaritan. There was really no other choice.

* * *

Warm at last, April wrinkled her nose as she pulled her clothes back on. The sweatpants were still wet, but she had nothing else to wear, so they would have to do. She stood behind the locked door, gathering her courage, trying to calm the voices that urged her to stay where she was. *Be real. I have to thank the man. He saved my life.* Drawing a steadying breath, she unlocked the door.

He was slumped in a chair, watching the television news, still in his coat—though it hung open now. At the sound of the door opening, he turned his head to face her.

April pasted a pleasant expression on her face... *Don't smile. Don't encourage him.* "Hi. Thank you for digging me out of the car."

As he rose from the chair, tall and broad-shouldered, she tensed, hand still on the doorknob, ready to retreat if he made a threatening move. She concentrated on his face, trying not to focus on the large, strong hand he ran through his unruly hair.

Dropping the hand to his side, he stood still, almost smiling. "I was beginning to wonder if you were able to speak."

"Oh. Sorry. I was really disoriented. It took a while to get my brain to function."

"Are you okay?"

"Yes, I think so. Thank you. I didn't..." She cleared her throat, and her voice tightened. "I didn't expect to wake up alive," she said quickly, then blinked away the hot tears that sprang into her eyes. She had to stay strong, be alert.

His posture relaxed, and he gave her a quick smile.

Warmth rushed through her body. *Oh my gosh.* The man was devastating when he smiled. *Steady, girl.* To take her mind off those feelings, she jolted into speech. "What's your name? And where are we? I don't know how far I'd gotten when I slid off the road."

He nodded towards the bed. "Why don't you sit down, and let me use the facilities? We'll talk when I'm done."

With a quick bob of her head, she perched on a bottom corner of the bed, ready to jump away if he tried anything as he passed her on his way into the bathroom. As soon as he shut the door, she moved around to the far side of the bed, scooted a chair over and sat down by the phone. *Who can I call?*

He hadn't done anything, yet... *Except save my life...* so she probably shouldn't call 911. Her mother was dead. There were other relatives in York, but no one she was close to. Besides, they were too far away to do her any good.

St. Louis was closer and she had a job lined up there, but she didn't know how far away she still was, and didn't know her new work number anyway. It was on speed dial in her cell phone. She'd planned on looking up old friends when she got to the city, but a call from out of the blue for help? Not a good idea.

No, she was on her own. But she stayed where she was. She just felt safer sitting close to the phone.

The sound of running water stopped, and the door to the bathroom opened. The stranger's eyes flicked to her. His lips lifted slightly as he sat on the mattress corner she had vacated. "My name is Max Moretti. I'm a biology professor, moving to St. Louis to teach at Gateway University. I've been driving for two days. I know I might not look it, but I'm one of the good guys, so it's safe for you to relax, if you want to." His eyes laughed at her as he smiled again.

She felt herself flush and smiled back, but stayed alert. His name was familiar... meant something, or reminded her of someone... but she couldn't make the connection. Probably it would come to her later. "I'm glad to hear that," she said.

Max nodded and leaned back, resting his elbows on the bed. Strange—she was scared—of him. *Be logical, Moretti. You outweigh the woman by at least sixty pounds and you've dragged her into a motel room with you. She doesn't know you. Of course she's nervous.*

Max shrugged, mentally. He could understand that. She was only average in height, and slim. But attractive… very much so. He ordered his body to stand down, and tried to look harmless. It was a shame she was afraid of him. Maybe later she'd relax a bit.

Dummy. You don't even know where she's going… if she lives around here… nothing. Stop getting ahead of yourself.

All right. First things first. Max smiled again, hoping it would reassure her. "Look, we need a plan. How about we call a wrecker to get your car and trailer back on the road, and then find some food? I don't know about you, but I'm starving."

"Well, yes, good. But where are we?" She shook her head, and red hair gleamed in the light from the window. "I mean, I know we're on Interstate 70 somewhere, but are we close to St Louis? I have no idea how far I got, crawling along in the snowstorm last night. And…" She hesitated, then looked him in the eye. "My purse and ID are all in the car."

He had the feeling he'd passed some sort of test. Maybe she'd decided to trust him. "All the more reason to get it back on the road as soon as possible. Why don't you call the front desk and see who they recommend?"

"Right." Why hadn't she thought of that while he was in the bathroom? *Brain dead, clearly.* "I was just about to do that." Well, she would have, eventually.

Luck was with her. There was a local garage that had a tow truck and they assured her they would be able to handle getting her car, and the trailer, up the hill without any trouble. "Oh, that's wonderful," she said in relief, and nearly missed the tail end of the sentence.

"… first thing tomorrow."

"Tomorrow? But it's early. Why not today?"

"Well, we might could get to it today, but we have a lot of calls that came in ahead of yours. Driveways need plowing; people need to be able to get out, get to work." The man on the other end of the connection seemed unconcerned about her plight.

April's voice rose a fraction. "I have to get somewhere too," she insisted.

"Ma'am," she could hear kindness in the voice now, mixed with a complete lack of compromise, "these are our regular customers. We can't afford not to take care of them. If we can get to your car sooner, I'll call you. Would you like to give me your number?"

"I'm at the Harvest House motel. April Windham is my name."

April Windham? Max's mind, which had been focused primarily on breakfast, jerked to attention. So the glorious red hair hadn't come from a bottle. He looked more closely at her as she set the phone down.

Her eyes remained averted and a worried frown creased her brow. He'd thought she looked familiar, but... April Windham. The hair was sleek instead of curly and her legs, which he had always thought amazing, were hidden by the baggy sweatpants she wore. He wondered if they looked as good as he'd imagined when he'd been a hormone-ridden twelve, and she'd been a stunning twenty-year old coed. Looking at her with new eyes, memories of a thousand teenage fantasies twisted embarrassingly through his brain. With a shake of his head, he tossed them aside. Her face was more refined than it had been—beautifully so—and she was slimmer than he remembered. But he couldn't keep his eyes from straying to those damn baggy sweatpants. As a youth, he had aspired to be a leg man, and in his imagination had gifted his dream woman with legs that had been perfection to him once— long, sleek and tanned—though in the entire fall semester when he'd known her, he'd never actually seen her in anything more revealing than boots and jeans. His interest in her legs now was just as intense, again a matter of curiosity, but fueled by a sudden spear of adult male lust.

She turned her head toward him to speak, and her brows jerked together.

Caught. He buried desire under an expression of benign friendliness. "Well, what's the word?"

The frown smoothed out, almost vanishing. "They say they can't do anything until tomorrow. I'll need to spend the night, but my purse, my credit cards, my phone—they're all in the car. She hesitated. "I don't suppose you stopped to lock it when you pulled me out."

As if he'd had nothing better to do! "No. I wasn't worried about the car just then."

"Of course. But do you think maybe..." She worried her lower lip and he nearly groaned. It was full, rosebud red even unpainted, and his quick mind projected vivid sensations of softness and sweetness, making his lips tingle and his mouth water.

"I hate to ask this, and I'll try to find another way, but if there's no taxi in town, could you possibly..."

He sighed. The time would cost him. He needed to get to St. Louis, locate the furnished apartment he'd rented and settle in. Lucy would be waiting to hear that he'd arrived. But what could he do? Knowing who April was, there was no way he could abandon her. And he had to admit he wanted to find out more about her... to see if the feelings he was having were just echoes of the past or if there might be something there worth pursuing. "Look. Let's get some breakfast. I can't leave you here. If I did save your life, that means I'm responsible for it now, right? We'll drive back out to your car and get what you need, then I'll be on my way—but first we get some food. Deal?"

She gave him a shaky smile. "Deal."

III

Outside the window of Gil Jones Realty, a chill November wind howled. April looked up from her desk and shuddered. At this rate it would be dark out when she left the building. Although it was nearly four weeks since she'd come to St. Louis, the accident she'd had while moving to the city still haunted her, making her nervous every time she had to drive at night. *It will go away, eventually.* In a few more minutes she could close up and head for her apartment. If she was lucky, she'd beat the snow waiting in the opaque white sky. She picked up the last of the folders she'd been working on, and rose to file them.

So far, this job was going well. The people in the office were nice, and her boss was reasonable. Business was slow, but she was content. She hadn't expected many sales to come her way yet. She used her time in the office to network online, making contacts that would serve her well when spring came and the market picked up again. And she had actually listed a few houses, despite the chill that an early winter put on real estate sales. Things were going as planned.

The outer door opened letting in a swirl of icy air. April turned with her professional smile in place, then stopped and stared. It was him. The man from the motel—the man who'd rescued her. She hadn't expected to see him ever again. What was he doing here? Max. That was it. Max-something. He was unwrapping the woolen scarf protecting his lips and chin, and pulling off his knit cap. Then he looked her way and the impact of warm brown eyes made it hard to take a breath.

For a long moment, April remained immobile, caught eye to eye. Then… *Talk!* She jerked air into her lungs. "Max. Mr. Mmm…"

As she hesitated, he spoke. "Moretti. Max Moretti. How are you Ms. Windham? Fully recovered?"

"Yes, thanks. I'm fine. And you? Is your position at the university going well?"

"It is." Without further preamble, he got to business. "I've been looking for a home to purchase, and I've found one that may suit my needs. Your name was on the sign."

"Really?" Her mind ran over the three houses she'd listed so far. None seemed to fit. "Wonderful. Which property are you interested in?"

"The Victorian on Alderdale Avenue. I'd like to arrange to go through it as soon as possible. I'm under a bit of a deadline. I have to be settled by Christmas—a little before then would be even better."

"Of course. The house is vacant. I'd be happy to show it to you. Will tomorrow afternoon fit your schedule?"

"Well… " He shifted his feet and tilted his head. "I had hoped to see it today."

April was a professional saleswoman, and a good one. Nerves would not be allowed to stand in the way of a potential sale. "All right. We can go there now." She shrugged into her slim thermo-lite coat, slipping her smartphone into the pocket. "Let's go through this way. My car is out back. Just let me lock the front door."

Knit cap and scarf in hand, he waited until she passed him and followed her out. Folding his tall frame into the passenger seat of her late model sedan, he listened politely as she gave him a quick run-down on the salient features of the property he'd chosen. He wasn't much interested in square footage or property taxes. He had gone online to survey the houses for sale in the vicinity of the university, and found nothing he cared for until he stumbled across this one, almost by accident, while taking a run during lunch. When he saw April's name on the sign he knew his instincts were right. He was *meant* to find her again.

And the house was perfect. He'd have been interested in it regardless of who the listing agent was. The old Victorian had bright paint highlighting its gingerbread trim, in authentic colors from the era. Someone had known what they were about when the home was restored—at least it looked that way. But the yard was seriously overgrown, and a large fallen limb lay across the path to the front door. He wondered what story lay behind the apparent neglect. Bored with April's recitation of facts, he interrupted.

"The house looks great, but why is the yard such a wreck?"

Her gray eyes flicked toward him. She looked surprised. Then she frowned slightly. "Well, as I understand it, the restoration was done by a young couple about three years ago. They divorced and the house sat until the court decided it should be sold—maybe it was a bone of contention between the two—I don't know. The listing only came to me last week. I was lucky enough to be on phone duty when the call came in. But it's a desirable property in an excellent neighborhood. You shouldn't let the state of the yard put you off."

"No, I won't. Doesn't the history of the place interest you?"

A small frown wrinkled her forehead. "As far as the disclosure goes, there was no negative history to be concerned about. The structural renovation was handled by a well-respected contractor and everything was brought up to code or beyond."

Her answer took him by surprise—and put him off. Maybe it was just as well that she didn't remember him. She was all business. Didn't the charm, the mystery, of the house appeal to her at all?

Brows drawn together in thought, he studied her face as she parked the car in the drive and led the way to the house. The April he remembered had embraced life with enthusiasm and humor. Had he been wrong? Had she changed so much?

It was warm inside. He looked at her in surprise and she grinned. "Take your coat off. The owners have kept the heat and AC on, out of respect for the house. It seems they still share a concern for their renovation, despite the circumstances."

The droll undertone in her voice reassured him. And, feeling more hopeful, he tossed his things onto a folding table in the entryway holding a stack of papers and cards from various realtors. April draped her coat over the back of a chair sitting behind the table, and handed him a fact sheet for the house.

"This stairway is one of the best features of the home," she said, gesturing toward a magnificent curved stairway. "Let's start on the second floor."

He followed her up the stairs. She was wearing a pencil skirt in a modest length, but his eyes were drawn to her legs. Not the sleek, tanned gams of his adolescent fantasies, they were pleasantly curvy and creamy white, as befitted her natural red hair. He was tempted to reach out and stroke one, certain the skin would flow beneath his palm like silk.

The legs reached the top landing and turned toward him. He raised his head and found a pair of generously curved breasts at eye-level. *Dammit, man. Stop acting like a fool kid.* He coughed. "I'm sorry. What did you ask?" He looked away from her, embarrassed.

"I asked if you were looking for a family home." Her voice was good-humored, almost amused. "This would be a wonderful home to raise children in. There are servant's stairs at either end of the hall—secret passages, if you will—and the end bedrooms have window seats in the cupolas." She led the way into the corner room.

"My daughter would love this room." The ceilings were high, with an old-fashioned chandelier dangling down. The corner cupola faced the upper branches of a sturdy tree. In one cleft a bird's nest still nestled, looking forlorn against the cold grey sky.

He imagined Lucy sitting, staring out the window at rain falling in the yard. There would be a cozy fire in the hearth and lace curtains at the windows. And Martha, her current baby-doll, in her arms. Unexpected loneliness made his throat tight and he cleared it roughly.

He turned to find April had widened the distance between them. *Better explain.* "Sorry." He tilted his head and shrugged, as if apologizing for his momentary distraction. "My wife died four years ago. It's been just Lucy and me ever since. She's staying with her grandparents until I get settled. That's why I have a Christmas deadline. I promised her we'd be together by then."

"I see." She smiled.

"What's the asking price?"

Taking a step towards him, she named a figure.

"Fine. I want it. Let's begin at 5% below their price, unless they have other offers on it?" His voice raised in question.

April shook her head. "Not so far as I am aware of, but I'll check of course." She frowned slightly. "Are you sure you don't want to look around first?"

He gave her his best smile. *Now, Moretti.* "Of course I want to look around. And the offer is contingent on a favorable inspection report. But when I find something special…" He let his eyes slide smoothly from her face to her elbow and back—just a quick glance, he didn't want to make her uncomfortable, only enough to let her know he wasn't *only* talking about the house… "I tend to move quickly."

The rose in her cheeks deepened a shade, and he knew she understood. She smiled up at him and his heart jumped into a higher tempo. "So I see." She turned and with a graceful swing of her hips, led the way to the next room off the hall.

Max followed with a spring in his step. *All right! Ask her, Moretti. You're on a roll.*

* * *

The next afternoon, April smiled as she sat at the desk in her apartment, checking her online listing pages. She hadn't had many hits from people visiting her internet site, but in two hours, she had a date with Dr. Max Moretti. She leaned back in her ergonomically-correct chair and stretched luxuriously, lifting her eyes to the apartment window. It was snowing today. Big lazy flakes drifted down through the bare branches of trees in the apartment courtyard. It was good to be back in St. Louis.

The older apartment building April lived in had been renovated rather than modernized, and the continued existence of the central courtyard and the massive trees it contained were worth more to her than the pools, exercise rooms and other amenities newer buildings offered. A little bit of nature went a long way toward settling her soul after a tough day at the office. It was especially nice on days like today, when she had chosen to work at home—she had no clients interested in venturing out on a cold, snowy day to tour houses.

She sighed as she pictured Max as he'd looked yesterday when he asked her out. Tall and broad-shouldered with his dark hair rumpled and deep brown eyes dancing, he'd taken her initial refusal without a blink. Then he'd put his hand gently on her neck and tilted her chin up with a whisper of pressure from his thumb. "Come on, April, don't be so formal. You know you want to."

She felt again the rush of heat through her body and remembered the brief struggle she'd had with her conscience—she suspected that he was too young for her—but after all, it was only dinner. So she'd set her misgivings aside. No sense in looking for problems that might not exist.

"You're right, I do." She'd smiled as she said it, and there'd been a sense of *deja vu* about the moment. His thick-lashed eyes had been mesmerizingly close—but he hadn't kissed her. She wondered again how old he was.

"Great. I'll pick you up at four tomorrow," he said. "Where do you live?"

She'd given him her address without a qualm. After all, the man had saved her life once, and she'd already been at a motel room with him. Laughing to herself, she rose and left the spare bedroom slash office, closing the door firmly behind her. It was time to get ready for her date.

* * *

Max looked again at the address written on the back of April's business card. Yes, this was the right place. The brown brick apartment complex had an old-fashioned entryway into a large snow-covered courtyard. He looked up at bare branches of winter-stripped trees silhouetted against a light gray sky that promised more snow to come.

This was a nice place, solid and full of character. That boded well for him. He'd been thinking about April Windham since he was twelve years old. Well, not really… but he'd known she was beautiful, and trustworthy and kind. And finding her again after all these years… it was meant to be. He hadn't been kidding when he'd told her he liked to move fast once he'd made up his mind, and his mind was set on April. He could rationalize the speed of it—after all, he knew quite a lot about her and her character, and he didn't believe her core values would have changed much over time—but he didn't need to. She had always been something special. Thank God, this time around the difference in their ages wouldn't stand in his way.

He opened the door to the foyer and straightened his shoulders as he pushed her doorbell. Today his campaign began, and his objective was clear. He would marry April Windham and live in the Victorian house on Alderdale with her and Lucy. When the buzzer sounded, he opened the inner door and headed up the stairs.

* * *

April took a last look at herself in the full-length mirror. Unsure where they would be going for dinner so early in the day, she had opted for a dressy pair of jeans with high-heeled English leather boots, a sage green silk shirt and a brown-on-brown striped menswear vest. Yes, it would be suitable almost anywhere.

As she opened the door to Max, his eyes widened and she saw crinkles in the skin at the corners when he smiled. "You look perfect. Are you ready to go? I'll help you with your coat." Without waiting for a response, he scooped her coat from the sofa and held it open for her.

April shivered as Max ran a hand around the inside of her collar as if to free her hair. Heat rose in her belly. She wondered if he was one of those naturally 'touchy' people or if the caress was deliberately intended to keep a woman on edge. Whichever, Dr. Max Moretti was the most promising male she'd been out with in ages. She smiled, mostly to herself. She couldn't remember the last time she'd had a fancy dinner out.

* * *

He took her to the zoo.

It was the last thing April expected, though her apartment was reasonably nearby. They strolled hand in hand past the exhibits, and saw many more animals than April expected. "This is wonderful," she said. "It feels like we're the only people in the world."

"We may be the only visitors in the park," Max responded. "Most folk don't think of coming here in the winter months, but I love it, and I think the animals enjoy having some company."

April nodded her head in agreement. "I came here once before in winter. It was empty then, too."

"Really. Who were you with?" White teeth flashed as he smiled.

"I was babysitting a little boy. It was his birthday, and his parents weren't going to be home from work until late—they had a faculty meeting or something. He begged and begged until finally I gave in. We had a wonderful time..." Her voice trailed off. Max was smiling, but his eyes were on her lips, and his hands bracketed her as she leaned against the railing by the mountain goat enclosure.

She took a breath to still her jittery stomach, and he lifted his eyes to meet her gaze.

His head tilted to the right. "Did I mention that today is my birthday?"

"Your...?" Remembrance came in a flash. "Maximilian was his name. Are you...?"

He grinned at her. "As ever was, but I'm glad I didn't have to beg and beg to get you to come here this time."

Her hand was already lifting to push him away. "Wait. You can't… I used to babysit you!" The pressure of her hand on his chest didn't move him back at all, but it did make her aware of how warm and firm a wall he made in front of her.

"I had a terrible crush on you then. Did you know?"

"On me? You were what, eight, nine?"

"Twelve." He sounded disgruntled. "I was small for my age. And you were in college, with glorious waves of red hair and a figure no girl in my grade could match." His mouth was moving closer.

April pulled her head back, laughing in disbelief. "You had no business noticing at that age!" Her voice hardened. "Is that what this is? Indulging a childhood fantasy?"

"Not at all. I grew up long ago." His arms wrapped around her, gently, but inexorably drawing her toward him. "Does this feel like a schoolboy crush?"

The touch of his lips was cool at first from the winter air, but warmed instantly as he kissed her firmly. God help her, this was definitely an adult kiss. Her knees felt limp and useless, but it was okay. He held her so tightly, her legs had no need to support her.

There was a coiling, writhing heat within her, and when her lips opened in surprise he took immediate advantage and slipped his tongue inside, touching, stroking, and tasting. Part of her brain was appalled at the kiss, and even more by her reaction to it. But most of her mind was simply lost, drowning in a swirl of hot sensation. It had been a long time since she'd been kissed, and she'd swear it had never felt like this. She found herself clinging to his neck and pulling herself tightly against him. When he drew back gently, embarrassment swamped her. "I'm sorry. I didn't—."

"Hush." He put cold fingers up against her lips, still holding her body close to his. "Listen to me, please. April, you never let me get by with anything less than the whole truth. You didn't just make it impossible to lie to you, you taught me how to be honest with myself." He dropped his hand from her lips and shifted to wrap that arm back around her. "Be honest with yourself now. I know you won't lie to me. So tell me, do you want me? Because I want you, very much."

April stood, her body warmed by his embrace, her eyes watching snowflakes swirl softly around them, and tried to make sense of the desires and inhibitions tumbling around in a jumble within her. He waited, unmoving, as she struggled to bring clarity and sense to what she felt. At last, she sighed, and felt heat rise in her cheeks. He'd asked for honesty, and she was trapped. "Yes, I want you."

"Thank God." He dropped his head and once again his lips played on hers, kissing her till she was breathless and trembling.

As she gasped for air and sanity, he bent and swept her up into his arms, moving towards the park exit with long, sure strides. "What are you doing?" Somehow she managed to keep her voice smooth.

"The park's closing. It's five o'clock. I'm taking you back home."

"You are?"

He gave her a swift, hard kiss. "I am. I'm going to carry you up to your apartment, and lock us in together. Do you mind?"

Her head reeled. This was insane. Her voice was nearly breathless as she spoke. "No… No, I don't mind at all." It was true.

IV

The mid-winter sun came in through April's window, waking her. She sat up and looked at the broad, muscled back of the man sleeping beside her. She stroked her hand gently over the curves, enjoying the contrast of her creamy pale skin against the darker background of Max's back. He had arranged for a colleague to cover his classes today. They were closing on the Victorian. In just a few hours, Max would own the house he'd chosen—the house that had brought them together.

April sighed. The last month had been like something out of a dream. Max had an efficiency apartment near the university, but they spent all of their free time together, mostly at her place. Max said his apartment lived up to its advertising—it was efficient, period—and he preferred that charm of her home. He made her laugh and liked to cook with her, though he didn't usually cook on his own.

Still, when she'd come home late last night, after a grueling afternoon of home tours, he'd had spaghetti, salad, and a glass of wine waiting for her. She sighed again. The man was too good to be true, and she was going to get hurt.

She'd fallen in love with him, fool that she was, and it would never work. It was too much to expect that he would stay with her. He'd find some sweet, young thing to marry and continue building the family he'd begun when Lucy was born. Once the house closed, he'd move into the big Victorian and get it ready for

Christmas, when his daughter would arrive—he'd already begun buying decorations and storing them at his apartment. He'd have family here again, and he would forget about her.

Well, one thing she'd learned over the years—there was no sense borrowing trouble. Today he was here, and she would do her best to set worry aside and just enjoy. They had planned a celebratory dinner at the Harvest Restaurant, renowned for its elegant atmosphere and local specialties. She could already taste the herb-cheese toast, the black bean and roasted corn salad, and the sweet, tender pumpkin bread. Deliberately focused on the delicious evening to come, April rose from bed and began the ritual of preparing for the day.

* * *

In Harvest's dining room, April leaned back in her chair rubbing the heavy cloth napkin between nervous fingers as she looked at Max across the table. He'd been jubilant at the closing this afternoon, but his initial elation had since been replaced by tension. Oh, he was smiling and as charming as usual, but April could tell he had something on his mind. She was pretty sure she knew what it was. Apparently he'd decided to make a clean break with her instead of just letting their relationship drift into slow oblivion.

She shifted restlessly in her seat. The certainty of what was to come had spoiled her appetite for the fine food and wine. She'd eaten, but more to keep up appearances than because she was enjoying the food. He was working up to the big break. She watched as he wiped his palms nervously on his slacks and gave her a tentative smile.

"April, there's something we need to talk about."

Her stomach tensed even more, and she wished she hadn't eaten at all.

He reached across the table and took her hand, refusing to let go when she made a half-hearted attempt to pull away.

"Now that I have the house, I'll be moving in as soon as possible and getting things ready for Christmas, when Lucy will join me there."

Again she pulled back on her hand, but his grip only tightened.

"You're hurting me."

"Sorry." He let go and she yanked her hand back into her lap. "April, I want you to live in the Victorian with Lucy and me."

She stared at him, unbelieving. "You want me to live with you and your daughter?" Her voice was incredulous.

"You'll like Lucy—she's a sweet kid—nothing like I was."

April calmed down a bit. "So she's six. And you want me to live in the Victorian with the two of you." Her eyes narrowed. "What are you looking for, Max, a babysitter with benefits?"

He sat back, a deep crease between his brows. "Babysitter with…?" Then his eyes widened. "No. Not even close. April, I'm trying to ask you to marry me!"

"Marry you?" April thought she'd been uncomfortable before, but this was both better and worse… to be offered what she'd dreamed of… but it was impossible. "I can't marry you!"

His head pulled back as if he'd been slapped. "Why not? Have I just been fooling myself about us? I know we haven't talked about it, but I thought…" He just looked at her.

April felt her heart break. She couldn't stand the hurt she saw in his eyes. "You weren't wrong, Max. I love you." It was the first time she'd admitted it out loud, even to herself. "But I can't *marry* you. I'm eight years older than you are. You don't want your daughter to have a grandma instead of a mom. It isn't fair to her or to you."

He scowled at that. "Eight years isn't enough to make you her grandma. And even if it were, I don't care. I know you, and I love you. I want to marry you. Tell me the truth. Don't you *want* to marry me?"

A powerful vision filled April's mind. She saw herself, white-haired and frail clutching Max's arm as a little girl with his eyes and hair looked at her in disgust. Her eyes filled with tears. Biting the inside of her lip, she shook her head. "No, I don't want to marry you. Please take me home." She kept her eyes on the table in front of her, waiting as he rose and pulled out her chair.

In silence, he walked her to the car and returned her to the apartment. "Good night, April." His voice was deep and distant. As she fumbled in her bag for her keys, he walked away.

"Good bye, Max," she choked.

He was already too far away to hear.

Swinging the door open, she winced at the emptiness of her apartment and the cold in her heart. Like an automaton, she locked the door behind her and walked into the bedroom. Picking up the t-shirt Max had discarded over a chair back that morning, she bunched it up against her face and curled in a ball on the bed, sobbing.

* * *

Two weeks later, April woke to the sound of a cheerful male voice. "—call us now and bring a Merry Christmas to one of the families on our list. We have many families of from three to five individuals still available, but our goal this morning is to get the larger families—those with six or more members--taken care of."

"And Bill," chimed in the female co-host, "we have a challenge! The swing shift at Monsanto is sponsoring a family of seven and challenges the day shift to match that. If you are on the day shift at Monsanto, don't let those guys on swing beat you… we actually have one family of eight that still needs to be sponsored."

"Great idea, Sandy! Call us at KXOK or drop by our website to sign up. Remember, all gifts must be delivered to the station by five o'clock on Christmas Eve. That only leaves nine days for shopping and wrap—"

April slammed the snooze button, then sat up and turned off the radio.

Moving slowly, she stumbled into the bathroom. Nine days until Christmas. She fought the temptation to simply turn back to the bedroom and curl up in fetal position beneath the bedcovers. She felt empty inside. Hollow.

Her mom was gone. It would be the first Christmas without her. And all her family was in Pennsylvania, not that she was close to any of those who remained. Here, where she had come to make a new start, she had... Max's face filled her mind's eye. She shut it out. Here she had no one.

She'd known things with Max wouldn't last, but she could never have guessed how empty life would be without him. *Come on. Snap out of it. It's not the first time you've lost a guy.*

Well, that was true. She'd been seriously interested in two men while living in York, and they'd both ended up married to other women. But it hadn't affected her like this. She'd been more angry, more frustrated, but she'd worked that off in the gym and jumped right back into dating. You couldn't catch anything with your line out of the water.

This time, with Max, was different. She'd never felt so old before, so hopeless. For the first time, she was thinking about living her life alone—permanently. She had no desire to date and no amount of arguing with herself had been able to renew her enthusiasm.

She swiped listlessly at the tears that puddled in her eyes and stepped into the shower.

An hour later, April headed toward her apartment door, looking trim and professional. Only another woman would have noticed the carefully concealed dark circles around her eyes or would think the slight dullness of her hair significant. As she paused to open the door, April's glance fell on the grocery bag against the wall. In it she had neatly packed Max's things. The bag had been there, mocking her, every day for two weeks. Would he never come by to get it? She couldn't bring herself to go by the Victorian or, worse, to seek him out at the university. Every time she thought of setting foot on campus, visions of young, fresh-faced coeds filled her brain. No, she wasn't going anywhere near that.

It's Christmas vacation. The students will be gone. She stood a moment, hesitating, then moving with resolve, picked up the bag and went out the door.

* * *

That afternoon, April narrowed her eyes against the cold glare of a low-riding sun as she surveyed the campus. *It must be beautiful in the fall.* Then the broad paths from building to building would be crowded with students, and the large expanses of glass bringing the outdoors into classrooms and offices would admit warm, golden light and views of trees ablaze in autumn finery.

Now, as April walked along an echoing hallway in the science building, the expanse of grey sky stared sullenly in at her, and skeletal tree branches mocked her loneliness. Near the end of the hall she saw the nameplate for his office:

Maximilian Moretti, Ph.D.
Associate Professor
Environmental Biology

Her hand moved as if of its own accord to caress the name. She snatched it back, and straightened to knock on the door.

"Come in."

A thrill shot through her at the sound of his voice. Pain followed swiftly after. Schooling her features into a neutral expression, she opened the door.

He was bent over his desk, sketching something, the top of his head facing her.

Her palms tingled and her stomach tightened at the memory of those thick waves against her hands. She swallowed her sudden panic and spoke clearly. "I've brought you your things."

His hand stopped moving, and his head lifted, staring at her with narrowed eyes. "Why are you here, April?"

She refused to shrink back at the censure in his voice. "I've brought you your things."

He rose and came around his desk, then sat on the front edge of it. In that position she found herself eye to eye with him, holding the bag of his things in front of her chest as if it were a shield.

He looked at her, his face empty of emotion. "You could have thrown them out, given them to charity. There's nothing of great value in there. Why are you here, April?"

Longing and need screamed for release. She clamped a lid on her feelings and, knowing they would break free if she stayed, spun about to escape, but the way was blocked.

A little girl stood between April and the doorway. A little girl with green eyes below Max's unruly hair, holding out a crayon drawing. On a hassock against the wall by the door, sat a pad of paper and an open box of crayons. April, completely focused on Max, had walked right past the child.

"I made a Christmas tree. Do you like it?"

Max's daughter.

April nodded, blinking away the tears that threatened to fall. "Yes, I like it very much."

"My name is Lucy."

"I'm pleased to meet you, Lucy. My name is April."

"You can have it." The girl held out the paper, unsmiling.

April set the grocery bag of Max's things on the visitor's chair in front of his desk and knelt down in front of the child. "Thank you." She reached out her hand to take the drawing. "It's beautiful."

"That's an angel on top. I don't know any angels. Do you?"

"Do I know angels? You mean real ones?"

A solemn nod answered her.

Unsure of where the conversation was headed, April responded with caution. "No, I don't think I know any real ones."

"My mom knows real ones. She's in heaven, so she gets to meet them." The green eyes watched April steadily, waiting for a response.

"Well, I guess if she can't be here with you, it's good that she's in heaven meeting angels. I'll bet she tells your guardian angel to take 'specially good care of you."

The child nodded in a matter-of-fact way. "Yes, she does. Daddy told me so. What's in the bag?"

"Nothing important. Just some stuff of your daddy's. Well, I'd better go." April rose to her feet.

"Where are you going?"

"I have to get back to work. I sell houses."

The child's face lit up with importance. "We have a house to sell! Can you sell our house?"

"You have a house to sell?"

"Yes. It's pretty and it's old. I like it, but Daddy says it's too big, so after Christmas we're going to sell it."

April frowned. She turned back to Max. He was still sitting on the edge of his desk, his head bowed. "You're putting the Victorian back on the market? Why?"

He raised his head just enough to look at her from under his brows. His mouth curved down. "It's a family home. It should have kids running on the stairs. Maybe a dog. Not just two lonely people rattling around inside."

"But then why did you buy it in the first place?"

He just looked at her.

Puzzled, she stared back, frowning.

After a long moment, his face went slack and he sighed heavily, not meeting her eyes. "I had plans." His gaze lifted to her face. "I never meant to live there alone."

Her heart stuttered in her chest. "Do you mean… ?"

He nodded, looking away from her. "I meant to live there with you."

"You meant… " She felt light-headed, uncomprehending. "From the beginning?"

His eyes turned toward her, narrow and intent. "From the minute you fell into my arms beside your snowed-in car. At first I discounted it as an after-effect of the adrenaline rush—the snow, pulling you from the car, carrying you up the hill. But when I heard your name, I knew I would find you again. I just knew it was meant to be." He laughed, a brief, bitter sound. "Guess I was wrong about that."

Lucy edged over to her father, and wrapped her arms around his leg, offering comfort. He pulled her up on his lap.

April's heart twisted. "No!" What had she been doing, walking away from his love?   "No. You weren't wrong. I was. I was afraid. I didn't expect you to love me. I didn't believe you could."   She reached to the side, groping for the back of the chair, and sank onto the edge of the seat. Her legs felt weak, and her mind exploded with possibilities she could no longer deny. The Fourth-of-July fireworks in her head made it difficult to think. She closed her eyes and searched for words. She looked at his knees, and Lucy's dangling feet. "I suppose if I can love you—and I do—then you can love me."

She searched his face, needing confirmation despite her brave words.

The ghost of a smile warmed his expression. "I do love you, April. Believe it."

"I do… I will…" She scrunched her lips as she smiled. "It might take me awhile to get used to."

His smile grew wider. "We'll give it some time. But for now," he looked at his daughter and winked, "would you like to go shopping with Lucy and me?"

What? "Shopping? Sure, that might be fun."

"Good." He looked at April, and she smiled back at him. Standing, he shifted Lucy to his hip, and wrapped his large, strong hand around April's fingers. "Then let's go…"

Snugged close to Max's side, his arm tight around her shoulders, April put her head against his chest. A weight she hadn't realized she'd been carrying lifted as she slipped her arms around his waist and hugged him tight. Tears of relief gathered in her eyes and trickled down her face. April sniffed, turning her head to blot them against his chest.

But a small hand reached out and wiped them away. "Don't cry, April. Come on. We're going to see the lights after we shop!"

* * *

"Three hundred fifty!"

April laughed along with Max and Lucy as they pulled into the driveway of the Victorian, past April's car, which she'd parked on the street. "I had no idea there were so many homes with Christmas lights between the Galleria and here."

"That was the biggest number yet! But our house is the best."

April looked at the Victorian, outlined in multi-colored strings of old-fashioned bulbs. She twisted toward the back seat. "I have to agree with you about that, Lucy. Your house is the best." She looked at Max. "Where did you get all the old lights?"

"They were in the attic. The couple that did the renovation must have been collecting them. Great, aren't they? Come inside and see the rest of the place. Lucy and I haven't had the chance to show it off to anyone yet."

"I'd love to." April stood waiting as Max unfastened Lucy's seat straps and lifted her from the car. They had taken a meandering route home, with side trips up every street where Lucy saw Christmas lights. Apparently it was part of the light counting tradition that each excursion *must* yield a higher number than the previous total. April was pretty sure Max had pushed the rules tonight when he decreed that the house down the street with lights on the garage counted as two, bringing them to three hundred forty-nine and making the Victorian a triumphant three hundred fifty.

"Can we have hot chocolate? Will you make cookies with us?" Lucy, sleepy but unwilling to give in, looked from her father to April.

Smiling broadly, April searched for a kind excuse—it was far too late to begin baking.

But Max intervened. "We'll make cookies tomorrow. I promise. But right now, we need to show April the decorations, and then you need to curl up in bed and go to sleep. Shall we start with the parlor?"

Lucy wiggled out of her father's arms and grabbed April's hand. "Come on, April. I get to turn on the lights!"

Max pushed open the polished double doors to the parlor. The tangy scent of pine stung April's nostrils. An eight-foot-tall noble fir didn't quite reach the high Victorian ceiling, but its girth dominated the diminutive sitting room.

April's eye's widened. "Wow."

Lucy flipped the wall switch and moved to stand in front of the massive, glowing tree. "It's pretty, isn't it? I picked out the angel for the top, and Daddy put it on. We hooked all the ornaments on together. I made this one. See?"

April looked more closely at the ornament indicated. It was located front and center on the massive tree—a snowman of

Styrofoam balls, with a black construction paper top hat and strands of bright purple yarn looped around the neck.

"I like it! Especially the scarf."

"Thank you. Would you like to see my room?"

"She can see your room in the morning," interposed Max, scooping up the child and heading for the stairs. "Just make yourself at home, April. I'll be right back."

In the morning.

April stood, watching Max and his daughter retreat up the stairs. Was she ready for this? Lucy had been open and friendly, but would that last?

Waiting for Max's promised return, she finally sank onto the antique settee tucked into a corner of the room. He was taking an awfully long time. In the quiet room, lit only by the bulbs on the tree, the emotional ups and downs of the day caught up with her at last. She kicked off her shoes, curled up her legs and leaned her head on her arm. Emotional exhaustion enveloped her, and April slept.

She dreamed of Max's kisses, warm and soft as she lay cradled in his arms, then drifted awake to find her dream was real. They were in the master bedroom, and she lay on smooth cotton sheets, still dressed, though she felt one of his hands beneath her head and the other at the buttons of her blouse. Sweet desire ran like warm honey through her veins, and her brain, after weeks alone, was awash in the sensation of his nearness. Shifting on the bed, she brought her arms around his neck, and relinquishing any hope of rational thought, lifted her mouth to his.

* * *

April woke to pale sunlight streaming through the straight lace panels covering Max's bedroom window. She arched her back for a luxurious stretch, then jerked to a sitting position, eyes wide. Max's bedroom. Where was he?

And where was Lucy?

Her gaze skittered around the room. Where were her clothes? The carpet, a well-worn Oriental, was bare. The chair in the corner held a bright silk pillow, but no clothes.

About to slip out of bed to investigate the mahogany wardrobe standing against the far wall, a knock on the door had her yanking the covers up to her neck.

"April?" Lucy's voice.

"Wait just a minute, honey." Desperate, she grabbed the man's pajama top tossed carelessly on the far side of the bed and slipped into it. Tucking the tails of the shirt under the sheets, she sat up straight, covers drawn to her waist. "Come in."

The door swung in. Max, grinning, held it open as Lucy entered, carefully balancing a breakfast tray complete with a sprig of holly sticking out of a pressed glass jelly jar.

"Why, thank you. How thoughtful of you to bring me breakfast," April began.

"Look at the holly," directed Lucy.

April smiled at the girl. "It's very pretty. Did you—?"

"No. *Look* at the holly!"

April drew her brows together—"All right."—and turned her attention to the sprig in the jelly jar. The light from the window reflected off the shiny green leaves and glinted... *Glinted?*

A square cut emerald flanked by diamond baguettes shone amid the leaves and berries.

April looked at Max, who stood behind Lucy, grinning like an idiot.

"It's not a Christmas present," Lucy informed her. "It's a ring."

"I... I see that."

Lucy looked at her as if April was hopelessly slow. "It's a marrying ring. If you put it on, it means you'll be my mommy here, and I'll have two."

Now April was confused. "Two?"

Max sat on the edge of the bed, blocking Lucy from view. "Two mommies," he said. "That's enough, Lucy. Let me take it from here." He took April's hands and held them sandwiched between his own.

She looked into his eyes, finding it hard to breathe.

"April, I love you. I want you to marry me... and be Lucy's mommy, here. I want you to be with me to watch her grow up. I want you to hold my hand when she walks down the aisle and remind me that we still have each other."

The reservations she thought she'd left behind began to crowd back at the thought of the years ahead. She withdrew slightly, troubled, but he only drew her hands closer to himself.

"And when we have grandchildren and great-grandchildren," he gave her a crooked smile, "I'll push you around in your wheelchair to visit them—or you can push me. Everyone knows that men fall apart earlier than women do." He gave her hands a shake. "Don't live a life of might-have-beens. Take the ring."

April looked at his hands gripping hers, warm and strong and sure. Lifting her head, she was caught by the intensity of his gaze.

"We need you, April. *I* need you. I will *always* need you. Come on. You know you want to." He waited, looking at her with warmth and love in his eyes.

April closed her eyes for a moment. He was right. She realized her hands had clenched into fists between his palms, holding onto her hesitations and her doubts. Bowing her head, she eased her fingers open and felt the silken cape of fear slip off her shoulders. For a moment she didn't move, then took a deep breath, free at last. As joy bubbled up inside, she smiled and opened her eyes. She felt a flush warm her cheeks. "You're right, Max. I want to, and I will." She pulled her left hand from between his and held it out to him.

Their eyes met and held.

Then a small hand grabbed April's and shoved the ring onto her forefinger. "There!" said Lucy.

Max slid the tray from April with one hand and grabbed Lucy with the other. "Not a romantic bone in her body!" he said as the two of them crashed on top of April, who opened her arms wide to hug them both.

Max lifted his head. "This is what I wanted when I bought this place. Not just a house." He beamed at them both.

"I wanted a home for Christmas."

Christmas a la Carte

By

Jeanne Kern

Dear Reader,

Recently I acted in a play in which one character was Madame Zelda, Fortune Teller--a charlatan for sure, but her good guesses made her seem magical. Some women have better intuition than others, yet if we listen to other people with interest and curiosity, we can all make good guesses.

I hope you enjoy this story, that you'll find your own "psychic powers," and that you'll visit my website (www.jeannekern.com) where you'll learn more about me and my book, *Destination: Love and Whales,* available in all e-book formats.

I foresee in your future a very Merry Christmas.

Sincerely,

Jeanne

"I don't want my fortune told. I'm hiring you as a personal shopper," Susan Albright declared, placing a twenty-dollar bill on the table.

Madame Zelda stared at her blankly. "Vhat do you mean?"

The terrible accent almost made Susan turn around and leave. The gold stretch turban was ridiculous, and the woman sounded like a cut-rate Gabor sister. But Susan needed help, so she planted her 2-inch heels that raised her to 5 feet 11 inches—sadly too tall for the average date, her lifelong sorrow—and stayed.

"I mean I'm hiring you. See, I have family coming to my apartment for Christmas. For the first time. It's all I can do to manage coffee and toast. In fact, I couldn't even do a turkey in my miniscule oven if I could do a turkey. Just sweet potatoes and bean casserole would strain my abilities and facilities." She tilted her head apologetically at the rhyme. "But in fact, sweet potatoes and casseroles won't do at all. It's my first At Home family gathering, and I have to look good."

Madame Zelda, she could see, was still blank and held up a defensive palm. "Vait. So vhat you vant ees a caterer?"

"No, no. Well, yes, of course I need a caterer. But that's not why I'm here." Susan unbuttoned her delicately hand-painted canvas coat and sat down. The Tums bottle rattled in her pocket as she leaned across the table, hoping proximity would make her audience more receptive.

"Everybody always talks about what everyone else gave them. They're very picky, sometimes abrasive, and my gifts disappoint every time. I simply can't think up what to buy for these relatives and I'm tired of feeling everything is all my fault."

"Let me get this straight," Zelda said. "You vant me to guess vhat you should buy as Chreestmas gifts? For people I've never even met?"

Susan shrugged and smiled. "I thought it through. You have to be a sort of psychologist to be in your business, so you ought to be able to figure people out. A personal shopper knows merchandise, but not people. You are a reasonable alternative.

"I'll tell you a bit about each person, and you tell me a present that might be appropriate. Can't be that hard—for someone who is good about people. That's not me." She held up her left hand and wiggled her fingers. "See? No ring. Everyone else in my family—both sides—was married before twenty."

She compressed her lips and stood up, walking two steps away as she said, "I'm the black sheep. Never mind that Mom had to raise us alone because Dad left her. My sister never sees her busy, busy husband. My brother makes his wife miserable. But they insist I should be married by now, which I would be if I ever met someone who didn't remind me of my own family.

"They don't get my work in television—keep telling me I should get a 'real' job. And they'll hate my apartment.

"Well, OK. If I haven't produced a date or a life they approve of in twenty-six years, I have to produce pretty great gifts." She turned back to the medium. "Won't you at least try to help me?"

Madam Zelda's gaze left Susan and lowered to focus on the twenty. "Eet's a long shot, dearie," she said. "I'll have to sharge axtra." Her head didn't move, but her eyes looked up to see her client's reaction.

Susan reached into her pocket and slapped down another $20. "I expected that. But that's the extent of *my* ability to figure people out." She sat. "There's a bonus if I love your suggestions. And I probably will, since I have no clues of my own. Let's get going." A reach into another pocket produced a folded page. Susan set that in front of Madame Zelda.

"Here are the names. My mother will be the hardest." Susan's voice broke on the word 'mother,' and the determination to act tough and insistent deserted her. "I can't believe I have to do this." Her neck and cheeks flamed, her shoulders slumped, and she clenched the edge of the table.

Madame Zelda's psychic powers might be questionable, but her compassion was quite real. She reached over and grasped Susan's tense right hand, held it in one of her own, and patted it gently with her other. "This isn't about shopping, is it, dearie? Vhat's really wrong?"

Susan shot a look at the psychic. Her accent was terrible, but her judgment was dead on. "You're right. It is more. I'm already stressing over what everyone will say. How they'll talk about their relationships as if they weren't nagging me about having none. And reminding me my job isn't 'real work.' I said I'm the black sheep; it's always been that way. I've always known they didn't really approve of me no matter how hard I ..." She broke off and fumbled in pocket after pocket, producing only another twenty which she dropped on the table.

To Madame Zelda's credit, she ignored it and produced a tissue with a flourish that was second-nature to her.

Susan mopped at her now puffy green eyes and blew her nose. "It's all so unfair," she hiccupped. "All my relatives have naturally curly hair." She tugged at a handful of her own thick but straight brown hair barely curving in around her neck. "And sports trophies. And families. And listings in Who's Who. Only me..." Tears overtook her again.

Madame Zelda slid the box of tissues to her, rose, and bustled into the kitchen. By the time Susan was calm again, cups of steaming chai were on the table.

"Now, then," she soothed. "I don't have to be psychic to see your hair's been professionally cut. You're vearing expensive clothes. You're villing to pay for vhat you vant. You must have a very good job. So if your family makes you feel inferior, I'd say dey're too mean-spirited to deserf any tears. Or geefts, for that matter."

Susan clutched her cup with both hands. "Oh, they don't mean to be unkind. That's what makes it so hard to deal with. But they all endlessly 'suggest' what I should be doing with my life. And the suggestions are more like dictates and disapproval about

Everything Me. And the gifts. Everyone is very judgmental about the gifts. I've used up all the ideas I ever had." She wiped her nose. "In fact, I seriously thought about running away for the holidays. Only I'd have to come back eventually. Because of my great job—you were right about that."

"Well," Madame Zelda conceded, "you're here now, so vhy not give eet a try? Let's see….I'll need you to tell me vhat each relative is like, vhat you usually give, vhat geefts seem to get high approval ratings. And I vant a story. You tell me von thing you remember about that person, interacting vith you or another relative. That might be enough. Maybe."

Susan took a gulp of tea. "A story? I don't know…"

"A story. I can't help you eef I don't have something to go on." The medium's accent fell away. "I can't take their hand and feel energy and aura; I'm kind of hog-tied here. Get going. Your $40 only pays for an hour, you know."

Susan cupped her face in her hands and pressed her fingertips hard against her temples where stress pounded. "OK. I wasn't expecting…All right. Let's start with Cassie. My older sister." The hands came down and Susan folded them under her chin, resting elbows on the red fringed tablecloth. "She's a socialite. Organizes big charity events. Micro-dermabraised, botoxed, and driven. Made sure her daughter got accepted into the best school and has the best nanny and takes French lessons and I'm sure she's already planning Kitty's—that's her 7-year-old—cotillion. She's nice enough, don't get me wrong, but there's no denying she's a snob. Has Kitty's birthday parties catered. With tents and entertainment. Always going to some big formal party. Alone sometimes, or with her doctor-husband when he can get away from the office."

Susan cocked her head. "She might be sort of lonesome. I've always felt sorry for her a bit. And Kitty. Kitty spends more time with the nanny than her mother."

Madame Zelda leaned in. "Vhat vas she like vhen you vere leettle?"

She seemed to have control again of that lame accent. Susan thought again about leaving. But, in for a penny, in for forty bucks. "Cassie used to be lots of fun. She'd come home from her ballet classes and try to teach me the steps. I could never get them right; I was gawky and always bumping into things. But she used to be patient with me. Then she got older and lost interest in me completely.

"She danced and sang a lot, and she started getting prizes and got swell-headed and unbearable. Until in high school when she lost the talent show first prize to Esther Jane Milligan.

"She never spoke to Esther Jane again. And the next day she gave me all her ballet costumes and quit lessons and never entered another contest."

Susan closed her eyes, remembering. "I played dress-up until the costumes fell apart, pretending I was graceful like Cassie." The eyes opened again, and she looked at Madame Zelda.

"She made what our family calls a 'suitable' marriage and works hard at being Known."

"And is she happy? Vhat isn't great in her life?"

"Oh, she complains a lot. Of course I only hear it at family gatherings now. But she goes on about caterers who don't deliver what they promised, florists who switch flowers at the last minute. Is that what you mean? I know she got mad at Kitty's French teacher when she taught the kids some slang expressions. Cassie didn't think that was 'appropriate.' And her husband works too many hours. And she can't lose the 25 pounds she gained when she had Kitty."

Madame Zelda reached under the table and pulled out a laptop. "Let me consult my crystal ball, here," she said, and her fingers flew over the keys. "Vhat's her address?"

Susan supplied the address, and talked over the clicking of computer keys. "I've given her tea sets, beautiful place cards, crystal vases, hand-wrought silver picture frames, jewelry. I can always tell she intends to return whatever it is as soon as she can."

Whirring announced activation of a printer in the corner, and Madame Zelda rose, swooped across the room, and picked up several printed pages.

"Von sister down. Who's next?"

"You've got something already? What?"

"OK, first, it had to be something she couldn't return. Next, anyone can guess she needs to spend more time with Kitty and remember she's a child. Third, she needs time away from her society friends. And fourth, she's overwei..uh, veight. This is perfect. But it's only perfect if you agree to some ground rules."

"Ground rules? I thought I was hiring you…"

"Ground rules," Madame Zelda interrupted firmly, planting her ample rear back in her ornate high-backed chair behind the table. "You have to recognize vhat is quite apparent. You care vay too much vhat your family thinks. You are an adult. Successful. Independent. Making your own decisions about your life and relationships. Adults do not allow themselves to be trapped into feeling inferior vhen they are clearly not. Am I right?"

Susan swallowed. Then smiled. "Right. I guess."

"Guess, nothing. You're single. That's fine. You'll change dat status when you choose. You're not a cook. Dat's fine. There are caterers out there eager for vork. In fact, I can recommend one for your family dinner if you vish. Gifts given graciously should not be appraised or criticized. If your family refuses to accept gifts for the good vill behind them, they don't deserve your thought and vorry. Can you agree to that?"

Susan blinked. Then smiled. "You're right. I'm so used to things being what they've always been—and I'm not that little awkward girl any more. Why should I apologize? Yes. I agree. With my head, anyhow." She exhaled explosively. "But knowing and believing…"

"Then here's the deal I offer," Zelda interrupted. "If you think I've chosen a perfect gift for your sister—if *you* think, not if *she* thinks, mind you—then I vill proceed to order all your gifts on line. You vill provide the credit card. Ve vill not argue about the other selections. Ve'll have things gift-wrapped and sent, so you vill have nothing more to do vith them after today. And you vill pay me $100. The $40 vill be part of that payment, of course. Fair is fair. Agreed?"

"But..."

"No buts. If you like vhat I suggest for your sister, I vill be in charge of your gift selections. You vill be in charge of growing up and acting like it."

That stung.

Madame Zelda was absolutely right. There was no reason to let her family make her feel like a slightly dim five-year-old. She was a successful businesswoman. If they didn't like what she gave them, that really was their problem, not hers.

"Yes!" she said. "Yes. You're so right. Damn the gift selection; full speed ahead."

Just knowing she wouldn't have to pick the presents was liberating. She'd thought initially having someone else to *blame* would be the major benefit of hiring a personal shopper, but this was way better. There shouldn't be any blame. No matter what her picky relatives said about the gifts, they weren't bad gifts, and she wasn't a bad person. So who cared? So far, her life choices had netted her a job she loved and an apartment that was small and funky but hers, and she wouldn't apologize for either. Hah! "Yes," she said again.

Madame Zelda passed her the cover of a brochure. The top line declared, "Do it for her. Do it for you." The picture showed a mother and daughter dressed casually, wearing ballet slippers and holding a graceful position. Underneath, it said, "You loved dancing as a child. Your child would love it, too. Why not do it together?"

"Mother-daughter ballet class? Oh, that's perfect. Kitty would be so happy to do anything with Cassie, and Cassie would get time with Kitty. How did you think of this?"

Zelda answered with a dismissive shrug. "My cousin owns the studio. Besides, I'm psychic, remember?" She stood and rolled up her sleeves. "If ve're going to tackle the whole family, ve need something stronger than chai."

They both laughed, and Zelda went into the kitchen and mixed a pitcher of margaritas.

Susan fished out another sixty dollars. Then she licked salt from the rim of her glass and downed her drink much faster than she normally would, wondering how to describe her younger brother. Zelda sipped slowly, occasionally nodding.

"Stephan—nobody ever calls him Steve or dares pronounce it like Steve-en a second time—was a cross-country runner until he got scarlet fever when he was 15. After that Mother coddled him. Made him spend hours in bed every day. Totally limited his outdoor time. Hired tutors. Reminded all of us over and over that Stephan was not healthy and must not be stressed.

"Maybe she was right, but Cassie and I hated it for him. And he hated it, too. His muscles all sort of punied up, and he got bookish and withdrawn. He's never come out of it. He's a hypochondriac. Wears coats and sweaters all year round. He doesn't ever raise his voice, and he looks like if he sneezed he'd shatter."

Zelda poured a second round. "What kind of gifts does he usually get?"

"As you'd guess, he usually gets sweaters, umbrellas, lap robes, gloves, brief cases, books. He sniffs when he says 'Thank you,' but he sniffs a lot anyhow." Susan shook her head and took another long drink.

"And a story, please."

"Story. OK. We were all very little, and Cassie and I read *Heidi*. Remember that? Remember the part where Heidi and the grandfather smuggle Clara out to the meadow and help her to walk again? Cassie and I snuck Stephan out to the park one day. He wouldn't run, but we played catch. And he had us push him on the swings until we were afraid he was so high he'd loop them. We stayed all day, had a great time, but Mother knew immediately because we all got sunburned. We all never heard the end of that. Good enough?"

But Zelda was already working the keyboard. She held out her hand. "Credit card?"

A worry slithered through Susan's brain: she was about to hand over her credit card to a stranger. "Oh, what the heck," she said, took another swig of her margarita, and gave Zelda the card.

The keyboard clicked. The printer whirred. Zelda looked up. "You said all your relatives were married. Stephan, too?"

"He married a practical nurse he hired to see him through what he thought was a bout of pneumonia. Marge is great. She keeps trying to pump some life into him. For a while she gave him B-6 shots. Or B-12. Whichever is supposed to give you energy. I don't know if she gave up on that. She certainly gave up on us. She never attends family functions. Smart girl."

"Here's to Marge!" Madame Zelda declared, and they clinked glasses and drank again. "Who's next?"

Susan wrinkled her nose and rolled her eyes. "This requires another dose of margarita," she said, and gulped the rest of her drink. "That would be Uncle Henry. Judge Henry Clayton Wharton, the Feared and Stuffy."

"Here comes the judge," Zelda groaned. They both laughed.

Zelda poured another round. "How many more?"

"Just Uncle Henry and Mother. Heeere's to Mother." Susan's lips felt thick. So did her tongue. And she felt thirsty. The salt on the rim of her glass must have dried her out. She took two large gulps of her fresh drink.

"Uncle Henry. Stuffy old Uncle Henny. Give him books about famous judges. Ol' Latin books. Canes and, oh, you know.

Umbrellas." Susan waved her hand extravagantly. It didn't feel like it belonged to her. "Gonna have a teeeensy nap." She put her head on the table.

And popped it up. "An' Mother. She's a micro-manager. Not a hugger. 'Sentiment doesn't get the job done,' she says. Busy, busy, busy." Susan rocked her head side to side with each "busy" and realized she shouldn't have. "Committees. Sooo many commit... She'll insist on very good food, you know. Can't keep a cook more than four months. Nobody good enough. She's a gour..." Her head went back down.

"Oh, for heaven's sake." Zelda pushed the computer aside.

"Aunt Zee!" A cheerful deep voice sounded from the back door. "Brought your dinner."

Zelda pushed back from the table and rose. "Tone it down a notch, sugar. We have sleeping company."

The doorway from the kitchen filled with six feet of Zach. And the aroma of beef and homemade bread.

"Oh, Aunt Zee. You've been ladling up your lethal margaritas again. You know this happens almost every time. Hey, this one's prettier than most—even with her mouth open."

"She's got a passel of stuffy self-centered relatives she's drinking to forget. Seems nice though. And hon, she's going to need a caterer for Christmas dinner for, as far as I can tell, five. Five people snooty about food. And, apparently, everything else, including this sweet girl. She can pay, so if you can squeeze her in, you might as vell get the job."

Zach laughed. "Vell? Might as vell? You're trying out that phony accent again? Just drop it, Zee. You stink at it." He gave his aunt a hug. "So. Christmas dinner, huh? What's the menu?"

"These people are snobs, remember? This girl seems to think she needs Baccarat crystal and silver chafing dishes and exotic food."

"So if I get the job, what do you think? Squid and pheasant and braised arugula salad with figs?"

"No, no. She *wants* that. Or thinks she does. But I say— give her turkey and gravy and cranberries and the whole standard American-as-apple-pie megillah. Including the apple pie. Rustic and simple and familiar as comfy shoes. And you count on that job. Now I've got two more gifts to order. Then we'll get some information from her purse, and you see she gets home and tucked into bed."

Zach took a closer look at Susan. "That will be a pleasure, Zee."

Susan awoke the next morning to light stabbing her eyes, knives slicing into her brain, and a body screaming for Novocain.

She managed to ease herself out of bed and, holding onto the wall, get to the kitchen. Her head flashed SOS signals and her teeth drummed with pain, but she got to the coffeepot. A note leaned against it. Mercifully large letters spelled JUST PUSH THE BUTTON. IT'S READY TO BREW. She didn't remember setting up the coffee. And why would she write herself a note? But she didn't want to think—her brain hurt—and she didn't really care. *Find the button. Push it.* That was all that mattered now. She lurched to the refrigerator and found bread. She stared for a moment at the butter and decided against it. No toasting either. Hard bread would be excruciating. Her mind hovered briefly on the word "toasting," but she let it go and used both hands to pour some coffee into a waiting mug.

She sat slowly, noting that even slow movement hurt. She dipped the slice of bread into the liquid and sucked the coffee out of it, letting the bread disintegrate in her mouth. It hurt. Lifting a coffee mug hurt. Blowing on the coffee because it was probably too hot, hurt. And touching her lips to the mug, hurt. But the coffee helped somewhat, and her brain started to wake up.

Note on the coffeepot? She never left notes on the coffeepot. She never set it up for morning, either, though she often wished she had. So how…?

And why did she feel this way? Was she coming down with some lethal form of flu? Had seven tiny miners infiltrated her bedroom and pounded their miniature tools against her skull all night? Had she been assaulted on the way home? Home…*from where*? What did she do yesterday? She lowered her gaze trying not to move her neck and discovered she was wearing her bra and panties. She sometimes slept nude, but never in her underwear.

Thinking hurt. She stopped doing it and slowly got another cup of coffee.

The phone rang. Sound really hurt.

"This is Zach," boomed the unfamiliar voice when she answered.

"Please. Whisper," she begged.

"Sorry. I'm Zee's nephew—uh, Madame Zelda to you. I know how you must be feeling; Aunt Zee laid you out with her margaritas, which could level armies. She's a great old gal, but she could kill people with one pitcher."

"Who…"

"Don't try to talk. Just listen. In your refrigerator, inside the door, is a Tupperware glass. Shake it, take the lid off, and drink it. It'll taste like chalk, but drink it all. Then just sit down. I promise it'll make you feel better in about half an hour. Just think of it as an old gypsy remedy, and drink it. Tupperware glass. Shake it first. I'll call again after you've recovered a bit. Now go."

She held the receiver to her ear until the dial tone made her jerk it away. Something was very wrong with what she'd heard. With everything, for that matter. She didn't know any Zach. Madame Zelda sounded a bit familiar, but she didn't want to think about why. Pain pulsed in her eyelashes and teeth. The coffee hadn't helped enough. Might as well…

Susan stumbled slowly to the refrigerator. She stepped on the loaf of bread she'd dropped on the floor in her earlier visit. There was, indeed, a Tupperware glass in the door shelf. "Shake. Drink. O.K." Taking no thought to what it might be or how it got there, she drank the mystery substance, chalky as advertised, and sat down. She rolled her head back, but that hurt, so she dropped her chin to her chest and waited. For death or feeling better, whichever came first. She really didn't care.

The doorbell rang. Susan opened her eyes, annoyed, and realized the sound hadn't hurt. She squinted at the kitchen clock and saw that time had indeed passed while she sat waiting for death. She eased herself upward and discovered it didn't hurt. She started for the door, remembering just before she opened it that she was nearly naked. The bell rang again.

"Just a minute," she called and dashed for her robe before admitting her caller.

Her tall, good-looking caller.

"Hi. You're Susan. I'm Zach Light. Your caterer slash set decorator. Assuming you still want dinner as part of the Christmas package courtesy of Madame Zelda. She of the corny accent but good heart. May I come in?"

She stood aside. Of course. Madame Zelda. Yesterday began to swim through her consciousness. Fortune teller. Red curtains. Something about Christmas. "You'll have to excuse me, uh, Zach. I am not myself and I'm not sure..."

"Zee's margaritas." He shook his head. "They really should be illegal. She won't tell any of us how she makes them so we can remove ingredients when she's not looking, and they're like rohypnol. That's why I'm here. To recap your yesterday for you so you can decide if you want to proceed with the plans. Maybe you should sit down."

He moved closer, put his arm around her, and moved her to one of the two chairs in the living room. "OK. Yesterday you visited a medium, Madame Zelda. That's my Aunt Zee. Zelda really is her name, believe it or not. She knew you didn't believe in fortune-telling, but you wanted to hire her to select and buy presents for four of your relatives. You told her they were coming here for Christmas dinner, and you needed a caterer, too. That's me."

He handed her a business card which she squinted at. Her eyes wouldn't focus on the small print, so she dropped the card to her lap and looked up at him again. She certainly could focus on him. He was tall. His tee shirt stretched over a muscular chest beneath his open parka. Black hair curled over his forehead, and she could swear his smile made her dizzy. But she'd been dizzy before he came.

"OK, I see you're still confused. Darn Aunt Zee. Look." He lowered himself to her level sitting on his heels. "You needed someone to buy presents for your relatives. You hired Zee to do it, which she did. She said you liked what she suggested for your sister, remember that? And you said you needed a caterer because your kitchen is too small to cook for five. I've looked at it, and you're right about that."

"When did…"

"Last night. I brought you home. Your address and key were in your purse, which, by the way, is on your dresser."

Susan bolted up and took a step toward the bedroom.

"Don't worry. The credit card is back in your billfold." He rose and stepped back. "And I was a total gentleman. Couldn't let your sleep in all your clothes, but I didn't break the bounds of decency. And I left you a concoction the family has developed to diminish the effects of Zee's hospitality. She must have really liked you. She never serves her margaritas to first time clients."

His grin sent a wave of dizziness over her again. Or was it just the effort of trying to keep up?

"Anyhow, Zee's fixed the menu. I'll provide table, extra chairs, plates and silverware and napkins and glassware—the whole ball of wax. All you have to do is agree to my price. And to help with accessorizing this apartment for the holiday. You don't even have a tree. So here's my contract. The price is here." He leaned in to point at the papers she took. The papers made her feel totally helpless and so did his proximity and the slightly musky scent of soap.

But the price, once it swam into focus, seemed very reasonable and well within her price range. "Yes," she said.

"You never told Zee the date," he told her, "so I'll need that."

"It's the 23rd," she said. Now that he'd backed away her concentration was improving.

"So we have two weeks. I'll need to shuffle some schedules. And we'd better start accessorizing. Now before you balk and assume some strange man couldn't possibly know how to decorate properly, I worked my way through culinary school as a set decorator and designer for three local theatres." He surveyed the room. "You'll need to concentrate on the living and dining areas. I presume you'll have them put coats in the bedroom, so we'll need some festive touches there. Luckily you're a bit of a minimalist, so we won't be needing to rent storage space for your personal clutter."

She stiffened.

"Look. I'm not critical. I really like this space and what you've done with it. And you don't really have personal clutter, that's all I meant. So we can shift the sofa over there, move these chairs for a conversation area and bring in another, a bit of space behind them for traffic flow, and we can put the tree by the window. You won't need much. Just some greenery and spots of color here and there. If we start now—or as soon as you get dressed—"

Susan's face went crimson. "I'm sitting here chatting in my robe." She dashed for the bedroom.

"-- we can do all the shopping at Christmas Central and be done in about three hours," he went on at boosted volume. "That will be one more thing off your list of stresses."

"Ready in a jiffy," she called.

And true to her word, in fifteen minutes she was pulling on her coat.

Her speed and transformation made Zach raise his eyebrows and whistle. "From margarita victim to this. Fastest recovery on record. Aunt Zee is slipping." He tucked her hand under his arm and off they went.

Christmas Central was a huge warehouse that, from October to January, was jammed with everything Christmas. Trees were sold in the lot beside it, so many trees Susan was overwhelmed, but Zach knew exactly what size would look best. "I think a table tree will stand on that corner table you have in the dining area if we move it. And there's an outlet right under the window so the cord won't have to be tucked away or covered. They have a nifty stand built inside a mock cloisonné pot, so you won't need a skirt, and after the holidays you can use it to hold a plant or gloves and scarves or put it by the door for wet boots. Now let's find some good-looking garland."

Susan let go of the notion she should protest or offer suggestions as her admiration for Zach grew. This man knew what he was doing, and she allowed herself to be whisked about the large area watching Zach select oversized candy canes, glass containers, miles of garland, bolts of red ribbon, and mini-lights for the tree.

She felt she'd been on an exhilarating carnival ride when Zach finally stopped, put his hands on her shoulders, and said, "Lunch?"

"His eyes are black like his hair," she thought. "And his hands are strong." She wondered what they would feel like against her cheeks. And, yes, now that he brought it up, she was hungry. And happy. She hadn't been in control of anything for the past two days, but her stress was gone. She was being taken care of. Family Christmas was going to happen and she wasn't worried any more. All she had to do was go with the masculine whirlwind beside her and have…

"Lunch." she agreed, and they went hand in hand to a coffee shop nearby.

"O.K. Ground rules," Zach said.

"Ye gods, Is there a family controlling-gene here? That's just how your aunt started."

"And you're breaking one already. No talking about Aunt Zee or Christmas gifts or your dinner party at all. We're already controlling all that. So I want to know about your job, your life, what movies you love, your music. And I want to tell you how I got interested in food, unusual props I've created for stage plays, and my bowling team. You first. What *is* your job and why did you choose it?"

They talked, laughed, ate, and talked some more. Susan found herself watching Zach's mouth forming his words, and she had to restrain herself from reaching out to touch that mouth. But she didn't want the words to stop, and she could tell he was really listening to hers. He made her feel safe. Important. Valued. They ordered more coffee and talked on and on. By the time Zach paid the check it was almost time for dinner. And they laughed about that.

"I don't know when I've been so relaxed for a whole day," Susan said as they headed for Zach's loaded van. "Your family must have a magic stress-relieving gene, too."

"We do know how to enjoy the moment," he said. "And special people in it." He stopped, smiled down at her, and lifted her into the passenger seat. She heard him whistling as he walked around to his side. "And now comes the fun of decorating your apartment. You can help, but I make the artistic decisions."

He also made it fun. They strung a garland along the crown molding and tied festive bows along it, working with a natural rhythm that made the work go smoothly. Only once did the work stop. Decorating the small tree, they picked up the same ornament, and Susan's hand tingled at his touch. Their eyes met when their hands did, and the ornament shattered on the floor breaking the spell of the moment. And itself. Susan went for a broom and dustpan, while Zach arranged candy canes in crystal vases. Together they added streamers of ribbon in the bedroom, kitchen, and bath. They ordered pizza and ate it standing over the sink so they wouldn't drop crumbs. They sang their favorite carols and talked and laughed. Finally, Zach surveyed the apartment and proclaimed it almost perfect.

"I'll fix the centerpiece when I bring the table and extra chairs. How 'bout next Sunday? I'll have everything set up so all we'll need is the food. Now, plan on dinner with me tomorrow. I'll cook for you. You can bring red wine. Just one more thing." He reached above the front door and planted a hook. From his pocket he drew a sprig of mistletoe and hung it slightly askew overhead.

Then he drew Susan to him and kissed her soundly. "What a day. Never thought much of Aunt Zee's powers until she put you in my life."

"Zach," she said tentatively. "I know I'll panic. Can you please, please be my date? Meet my family and hold my hand? I'll need moral support."

"Thought you'd never ask." He kissed her again and was gone, leaving her stunned and amazingly happy.

Susan was rested and calm when the doorbell rang. "This'll be Cassie," she called to Zach supervising in the kitchen. "She's always first. That way she can control other people's arrivals so nobody else can make a grand entrance." Zach laughed loudly. For the first time, Susan found Cassie's need to control funny. And rather endearing.

She opened the door, and Cassie squealed and enveloped Susan in a hug.

"You darling!" she shrieked and held Susan at arm's length. "How did you think of it? Oh, how I've missed dancing, but I never realized. And Kitty adores it. We had our first session yesterday." She hugged Susan again before letting go and striding toward a chair. "When the gift card for ballet classes came, I thought about throwing it away. But Kitty was there asking what it was, and when she saw the brochure—well, I had to call for our first class that minute. And it was wonderful. Oh, I was sore this morning, but a nice hot bath took care of that. We can't wait for our next class. You are an angel!"

"I just remembered how graceful you've always been. And how you used to try to teach me."

"I know. You tried so hard. Oh, when I read your sweet note it all came back to me."

Sweet note? Susan frowned. *What sweet note?* But Cassie was just getting warmed up.

"So many things about when we were little. Remember when Cook let us make cookies and Mother saw the mess we made in the kitchen? But about the class. You won't believe it. We started barre exercises, and I couldn't get my leg high enough. Madame Zizi said I was very graceful and that most mothers take a couple of sessions before they limber up.

"But there was one mother who was, well, to be very kind, tubby." Cassie rounded her arms indicating a massive stomach. "And really out of shape. She could scarcely do a plie and straighten back up. Cute little girl, though. She and Kitty started talking after class. And you'll never guess who the mother turned out to be. Esther Jane Milligan! From high school! We all went to lunch, and I don't know why we drifted apart. We have so much in common. Her husband was always busy, too. And she divorced him." One of Cassie's perfectly formed eyebrows went up.

"Great present! And I have you to thank. But one thing puzzled me…"

Whatever Cassie wanted to know was cut off by the ringing of the bell.

"Zach," Susan called, "It's moral support time."

Zach emerged from the kitchen. His white shirt emphasized the olive skin and his black hair. Half-rolled sleeves emphasized his muscular arms. Cassie gaped, at an unprecedented loss for words.

Susan opened the door—to be crushed in a bear hug. Her brother let her go and stepped into the room, his surprisingly open coat swirling as he turned, inhaling deeply. "Smells like Christmas!" he observed.

"And you made Christmas for me." He turned back to Susan. "I couldn't believe it when I opened the packet. I thought it was some sort of cruel joke. Then your note fell out. Well, reading how you remembered my racing days and my love of speed, so much came absolutely flooding back. I've tried not to think of those days ever, but that *you* remember—well, I was flabbergasted. And touched. And delighted. I started to tell Marge about it, and I showed her your gift. She instantly started to plan when and how we could go."

He paced in obvious boyish excitement. *"Almost 200 miles per hour*--I can't wait! Marge called the number, and we had 20 tracks to choose from. *Six hundred horsepower.* It's too great!"

Stephan stopped mid-pace, noticing his other sister. "Oh, hi, Cassie. You know what this wonderful sister has given me? Speed! That's what. She's sending me to the Richard Petty Driving Experience. I'm going to drive a NASCAR racer. Marge is going along and we're going to buy her a shotgun ride with a real race driver." He grinned and flipped an imaginary Groucho cigar. "Of course whoever that is, he's no Stephan Albright. I feel like a kid, excited about Christmas again."

He swept Susan up in another hug and laughed. Only then did he notice the stranger.

"Congratulations, Mario Andretti. Sounds fantastic. I'm Zach; I'm with Susan." The two men shook hands heartily.

Susan couldn't remember Stephan's ever doing anything heartily. Or happily.

Zach poured drinks, and while Cassie tried to tell Stephan about her present, the bell rang again.

Susan opened it. There stood Judge Henry Clayton Wharton. Or rather, there leaned Judge Henry Clayton Wharton, balancing on a cane, his left foot encased in a bulky cast.

"Oh, Uncle Henry," Susan said, "what happened? Oh, come in, come in and sit down." She reached for his arm.

"Don't fuss," he ordered, shaking off her hands. "I can manage just fine with this thing." He brandished his cane and then stumped across the room. "You can take my coat and hat," he told her as she stared horrified at the cast.

"Let me, sir. I'm Zach." Zach was able to keep the judge upright as he struggled to shed the bulky outerwear.

"I'll sit down now, young man." Zach helped ease him into a chair. He pulled a cheerily wrapped box from beneath the tree and propped the cast on it.

"You can't crush this, Judge Wharton," he assured the uncle. "It's just a decoration. Only for looks. But it makes a serviceable footstool."

"Now, Uncle Henry, what happened?" Cassie demanded.

"Hello to you, too, Cassandra. Stephan. And Susan, my Christmas angel. This is your fault, you know. You and your Christmas present."

Accusing eyes turned to Susan who stood mystified.

Henry began to huff and squeak. Zach stepped toward him, clearly thinking "Heimlich," but the judge waved him off. Slowly they all realized he was laughing. They looked at each other, baffled. Uncle Henry laughing was totally new territory.

Finally the odd noises died down, and he said, "So far only Susan knows what I'm talking about. Only fair to share. Day before yesterday, a package arrived for me. Inside was a note." He produced a card from an inside pocket and read. "'Dear Uncle Henry, I made a marvelous discovery on the computer. When you were at Pembroke Prep, you captained the speed skating team. And one of your racing records still stands. You never told us this, but I am so impressed. The school website even has a photo of you in the sports archives section. There you are, slicing across the ice bent low and fairly zooming. I wanted to show how impressed I am and to remind you of that time in your life. Merry Christmas'."

"Skating champion?" "Record holder? Uncle Henry!" Cassie and Stephan blurted. It was all Susan could do to stay mum.

"Inside the package was a pair of skates." He turned to Susan. "How you knew my size I'll never know. But there in my hands was my youth—those happy years at Pembroke. Halcyon days with no responsibilities, packed with friends and fun. Well, it doesn't take a genius to figure out what I did." He thumped his cast with the cane.

Cassie started toward him, saying, "Susan, how could you?" He raised the cane to block her.

"Do *not* go fussing. I did this myself. No fool like an old fool. But oh, my, how good it felt to be foolish again. I wobbled on that ice for the first five minutes, but then some sort of muscle memory took over. I got my ice legs, and I picked up speed. People stopped to watch me go. I made it across the rink and most of the way back before I realized I should have begun to stop. And then suddenly..." the wheezing sound started again... "I stopped. At least the bottom part. The top part kept going, and I heard a snap. Darn ankle went. But, Susan, girl, I'd do it all again. What fun that was. Haven't felt like anything's been an adventure in years. Best Christmas present ever!"

Everyone beamed at Susan.

"Just one thing. There was this little business card inside. Who the deuce is Zelda Light, Personal Consultant?"

Susan, eyes wide with surprise and panic, looked at Zach who struggled to fight back a laugh.

"Yes," Cassie said. "Who is that?"

"I had one of those, too," Stephan added. "And where's Mother?"

As if on cue, the doorbell rang. Somehow the chime managed to sound demanding. A sharp knock followed immediately.

"There's her patient little self now," said Uncle Henry. He was still smiling.

Susan opened the door, and Rita the Matriarch swept in, air kissing. "Stephan, happy holiday. Cassie, merry Christmas. Henry, whatever did you do to your foot? And who," she asked stopping in front of Zach, "is this?"

"Zach Light, I'm with…"

"Delight! You're from Delight." Her elbow-length glove fluttered to his chest. "Susan, how did you nail the busiest caterer in town? And the best!" She turned a neon smile on Zach. "Are we actually to be treated to a Delight meal?"

"I did cater the dinner. But today I'm Susan's date."

"Date? Susan, do you have any idea? Years without, and suddenly…. Do you realize this is one of the Top Ten Bachelors in this town? On the latest list? Of course you don't. You never read society magazines. Mr. Light, I am, well, delighted. And we'll be seeing more of each other." Her eyes twinkled. "I'm going to be one of your students, thanks to your date here."

She turned, playing to the room as her avid audience. "Susan has given me cooking classes at Delight. Cooking! Me! Can you imagine? She said she knows how I've suffered with incompetent cooks, and she wanted me to study with the best so I could control special meals myself. What a good idea." She turned back to Zach. "And you surely are the best, Chef Light. Everyone in town simply raves. I promise to be a good student and practice religiously."

Zach moved to Susan's side. "I believe dinner is served. Tonight we celebrate Family with an old-fashioned traditional Christmas dinner. As my Aunt Zee says, 'Families should be together, and Christmas dinner should be familiar as comfy shoes. You remember those, Judge?"

Cassie and Stephan froze, waiting for a judicial ax to fall.

Uncle Henry took Zach's arm to lever himself up. He stared into Zach's eyes for a long moment. Then he wheezed in laughter again and slapped Zach on the back. "Good joke. Welcome to the family, son. Once Rita gets her clutches on you there's no escape."

"I don't think I want to escape," Zach said. "This is the best Christmas I've had yet." He tucked Susan's arm in his and bent to her ear to whisper, "Aunt Zee gave me the best gift ever, too."

Susan beamed as they followed her family toward the welcoming table. "Me, too. She gave me my family the way I always hoped they could be. And she gave me you. Every gift a gold star." She stopped suddenly and whirled to face him.

"Good heavens, Zach. It's true. Zelda really does have psychic powers."

The Christmas Gift

By

BJ Akin

Dear Reader:

In the Sandhills of Nebraska, we aren't so comfortable talking about ourselves and tend to let our work speak for itself. So you jump right on in and read *The Christmas Gift*. It's a good story and, if you read between the lines, you'll get to know a lot about me as well.

You may get in touch at sandhills.dreamer@gmail.com. Watch for the future release of "Sandhills Dreamer," a full length historical western romance based in the Nebraska Sandhills. I wish you the best holidays ever!

Welcome, and enjoy!
~ BJ

CHAPTER 1

Waving goodbye, Rebecca smiled at the two children as they rode double on their old black mare, heading west out of the schoolyard. They were the last of the schoolchildren going home for the holidays. It was the day before Christmas Eve, and the little country school would be out for the next two weeks. Rebecca had started her first year of teaching at the Sandhill Valley School and was proud of her efforts with the fourteen schoolchildren. They ranged from the first grade up through the eighth. Most of them were quick learners, and even though she was new, they hadn't given her much trouble. At least nothing out of the ordinary, but she had only been here since early November when the last teacher had taken ill. He was an older gentleman who had taught there many years and decided to retire when his health improved.

This would be a quiet kind of Christmas, Rebecca thought, as she carried in extra wood for the night. She had all the things she would need for the upcoming weeks: food, water, and wood to keep her warm. And she certainly had plenty to do to pass the time. There were lessons to plan, books she had wanted to read and her embroidery.

As Rebecca went out the door, the wind tugged at it, almost pulling it out of her hand. She intended to get one more armload of kindling in case she needed to restart the fire during the night. Maybe I had better go feed and water Wrangler now, before it gets totally dark out and the wind gets worse, she thought, pulling her coat tighter. Wrangler was the sorrel filly she had purchased when she moved out here to the Sandhills of Nebraska to teach.

Most schools were located in small towns, but Rebecca's little grade school was out in the country, and she lived in the back of the building. There was an added room that was large enough to include a small table and a couple chairs, a sitting area by the fireplace and a bed in one of the corners. There was even a beautiful cedar wardrobe and chest to put her clothing and other things in. She kept her embroidery items in the chest, which protected them from moths and bugs. Someone had spent a great deal of time crafting the pieces. Anyone could see the expertise and love that had been carved into the wood. She had been told that one of the fathers of her students, a Mr. Bonner, had made the chest and wardrobe, though she had never met him. And now that she stopped to think about it, she wondered why she hadn't. All the other parents of the school children had come by at one time or another since her arrival to introduce themselves, allowing her to match the school children with the parents. She wasn't quite sure why, but Mr. Bonner, a widower, had not taken the time to visit her at the school. His children were six and ten, the youngest, a girl named Annabelle, and William the oldest, a boy. Both children were quiet, but the little girl spoke only when spoken to. The lad was a little more outgoing. The pair always rode their old black mare to and from school together but were never accompanied by their father.

When she first came to the school, she would see William gazing out the side window with such a forlorn look, and she worried that something was wrong. Once she had asked him at recess if he was all right or if there was something she could do for him. He must have been off daydreaming, because he didn't respond to the question at first, so she asked him again. Turning to look at her, his face had such a lost look that she felt a twinge of pity for him. He shook his head, said he was "fine" and "no," there wasn't any problem. But he turned right back to the window and continued to stare out into the cold light of day.

Rebecca knew she had to do something to remove that look from William's face and help Annabelle open up more. So after a couple days she came up with a plan. She knew that every young child likes animals and especially ones that could perform tricks. So every few days she would bring out her horse, Wrangler, and teach her a new trick. The whole school was amazed at how fast the horse learned. Rebecca could see a change coming over the two Bonner children in the next few weeks as she taught the horse new things. They were beginning to be more animated and talkative, not only with the other children, but also with her. She felt that she was finally earning their trust and respect more every day, and recently, Annabelle had taken to sitting with her at lunch time.

When the weather broke, maybe she would go visit with Mr. Bonner and try to learn more about the children so she could help them as she felt drawn to them in a way unlike any she had ever known. That would be a task she could accomplish after Christmas, Rebecca thought as she dusted off the pieces of bark still clinging to her coat and mittens. But for now she needed to finish up the rest of her chores before dark. She still had to carry water for Wrangler, feed her some grain and hay, and then she would need to carry in her own water for the night.

Stepping out into the increasing wind, Rebecca latched the shed door and headed back to the schoolhouse and her warm little room. She noticed the snowflakes swirling in the wind, and it felt much colder than it had when she first started her evening chores. Hurrying her footsteps, she gained the living quarters' door and welcomed the warmth of the room. Leaning against the door, she wondered, could it be a big storm coming or was it just her imagination because she was here alone and this would be her first big snowstorm? Oh never mind, she thought, I am just imagining the worst. It's just a little snow, nothing unusual about that! Heavens! It's winter!

Rebecca busied herself preparing supper and making some tea so she could sit by the glowing fireplace and bask in the heat. She would do some reading after supper and go to bed early as she had lots of things she wanted to do tomorrow during the short hours of winter daylight.

During the night Rebecca awoke and put more wood on the fire to keep it burning, keeping the chill off of the room. She thought she could hear the wind blowing much harder than when she had retired earlier that evening. She couldn't see anything out of the small window by the door. There was no moon, and the cloud cover would have hidden it even if there was one, she thought. Turning back and climbing into bed, she snuggled under the heavy quilts, thankful her mother had made her bring them and the fluffy feather tick! It held the heat of her body and kept her warm even on the nights she didn't wake up and stoke the fire with more wood.

In a few moments she was sound asleep, not noticing the increasing wind, plummeting temperature and increasing snowfall.

CHAPTER 2

At first Rebecca thought she was dreaming, hearing sounds of the ocean crashing on the rocks at the lighthouse where she had grown up in Maine. There was an explosion of sound like the waves and then she heard a soft keening sound. *Something wasn't right*!

Opening her eyes to the dimly shadowed room, Rebecca's senses were running wild. The fire was out and there was only a dim gray light coming from the window by the door. Rising from the warm bed, she pulled on her heavy robe and put her stocking feet into her winter boots, anxiety raising the hairs on her neck and arms. Walking over to the door, she unbolted the heavy bar and sucked in a deep breath before pulling on the wooden door handle.

Dumbfounded, she stood looking mutely at the solid wall of snow blocking the doorway. Panic rose in her throat choking off her breath. Unconsciously, she reached her hand out to the cold white wall of snow. "Ohhh!" She gasped. Touching the icy snow scared her even more. *What if she couldn't get out?* She had only brought in enough wood for last night's and today's fires.

And Wrangler needed to be fed and watered! She couldn't be blocked in the schoolhouse! Stepping back, Rebecca closed the door and slumped against it, trying to gather her thoughts on what to do first. She never imagined that she could get snowed in and not be able to leave the schoolhouse! Quickly she turned to look out the small window, but it was white with packed snow, giving her no signs of how thick it might be. Going over to the connecting door to the school classroom, she pushed frantically at the handle, rushing through to the dim classroom. There were only four windows, all were white, packed with snow, letting in just a little gray light. Rebecca had no idea what time of day it was right now, but guessed she had slept later than normal.

Taking a deep breath and pulling her heavy robe even tighter, she turned back toward her living quarters. Once inside, she closed the connecting door. Her mind started to race, recalling the years in Maine and all the snowstorms she had been through with her family there. That was the crux of the problem, she had been with her family. Her father and brothers had dug them out, taking care of the livestock and helping neighbors needing assistance in dealing with the heavy snowfall. But, her family wasn't here and she was on her own.

First things first, she thought, heading for her beautifully carved wardrobe. I'll get dressed, start the fire and get prepared to start digging. Then she remembered she had left the shovel in the barn last night when she took water to Wrangler. Oh never mind that, she thought, I should be able to find something to dig with from in here.

Soon she was attired for the cold weather, laying out heavy mittens and her coat for when she broke through the snow to the outside. Grabbing her tin washbasin, she headed for the door leading to the outside. Pulling it open and blocking it with one of the kitchen chairs, she vigorously started dipping her basin into the snow and throwing it in the corner farthest away from the fireplace, knowing that when it started to melt, it would create a watery mess.

Over an hour later, Rebecca sucked in an exhausted breath, pausing to look at the mound of snow then back at the small distance she had eroded into the snowbank. She tried shoving the broom handle up through the snow above her head hoping to feel the easy give when she broke through the surface, but she didn't feel any freeing of the pressure from the snow. She continued digging with the washbasin for another hour or so, but was becoming tired and hungry.

Turning back in toward her room, she walked the few feet of the footpath she had carved into the snow bank. Sighing, she closed the door and slumped tiredly against it. Rebecca looked over at the pile of snow in the corner and it dawned on her that it hadn't melted. She had been so intent on getting a pathway cleared, she hadn't thought about the fire dying out. It completely slipped her mind. She wasn't cold because she had worked up a sweat digging in the snow. Now she wondered if she had made a vital mistake.

Rebecca hurried over to the fireplace, laying out some kindling, dried moss and a few small pieces of firewood. Before she struck the match that would light the small fire, she said a silent prayer, remembering what her father had always said to do in the winter during a storm. "Never let the fire go out, daughter, because the heat keeps the chimney free of snow and keeps you warm so you can survive!" *She only hoped she wasn't too late!*

As the flame from the small matchstick flickered to life, Rebecca touched it to the dried moss, holding her breath as it ignited the small kindling. As the flames slowly traveled through the little twigs into the larger pieces of wood, Rebecca watched with hope as the larger pieces ignited, guaranteeing the fire was solidly lit.

Setting back on her heels, she stood up, her stomach growling with hunger. She was ravenous! Walking over to her nightstand, she picked up the watch pin her mother had given her upon her graduation. It read 10 o'clock. She wound it up and placed it back on the stand, remembering the day she had told her parents she had wanted to go West to teach and the family commotion that had erupted.

Her father had laughed, embraced her and smiled, saying she was following in the family tradition, exploring new lands, creating a life for herself. Three of her brothers had teased her, saying, "What would a little girl like you do out West?" The fourth had hugged her and whispered, "Way to go, sis. You'll do fine! Maybe, you'll invite me to visit?"

Her mother had clasped her tightly, her eyes filling with tears, "I hate to see you go so far away from home. What if something happens to you? Rebecca, you are my only daughter. But I can see your mind is already made up. May God go with you."

Rebecca hugged them all back, and assured them she would be just fine. She had trained to be a teacher, and the West certainly needed more teachers; she promised to write home regularly.

Now, here she was, several months later, and she sure could have used some help from her brothers dealing with this snowstorm! She didn't actually know how bad the weather was because she couldn't get outside!

Moving around the small kitchen area, she prepared a pot for tea and a piece of bread and butter. Then she began pulling out the few kettles and pans that were available to start melting snow. Walking over to the huge pile in the corner, she filled everything and set it close to the fireplace to melt. As it melted, she refilled each with more snow, giving her more water and depleting the pile of snow in the corner. After the first round of filling the pots and pans, she sat down by the fireplace to drink her tea and eat a little food, knowing she had to ration what she ate because most of her food supply was out in the storm cellar by the barn. Normally, she kept only a couple days' food supply inside. There wasn't any way to keep things fresh inside when there were warm days. Most food was stored in the cellar, including the smoked meats for winter consumption. She had forgotten to bring in a supply after school the previous day, so it had been almost four days since she had brought in fresh supplies. There wouldn't be a shortage of water, she thought, looking at all the pots. She worried about Wrangler in the barn even though she knew she had given the little filly enough for a couple days, but it might be longer before she could get to the barn.

CHAPTER 3

Even though her hair was thick with winter growth, the little sorrel filly shivered as she trudged through the steadily falling snow. Wrangler wasn't exactly sure why, but the memory and occasional scent of the old black mare kept pulling her forward. They had shared the corral with a few other saddle horses, but the two of them had seemed to hit it off and become friends, never biting or kicking like the other horses. Spending their day standing like old companions, eating and drinking together, watching the others without interest in getting involved in the constant one-upmanship that seemed to be a daily trial with the other horses.

As she approached a small creek, Wrangler looked about hoping to see the old black mare, but all she could see was white blowing snow. Cautiously she walked across the snow-packed frozen surface, lifting her feet and stepping down slowly, letting instinct guide her across. Once she reached the other side, there was a stand of large cedar trees, and she shouldered her way into the branches, hoping for a respite from the howling wind. Finding a spot out of the direct blast of the wind, Wrangler stamped her feet to knock off the big clumps of frozen snow. After the snow came off, she felt ready to go on.

Carefully she maneuvered her way out of the thick branches and continued to drift west as the wind continued its onslaught. The little filly put her head closer to the ground, picking up a breath of scent of the mare and on she went.

Later that night Wrangler drifted into the yard of the Bonner Ranch. She could hear sounds of other horses inside a solidly-built barn, turning her in that direction. Stopping by the big barn door, Wrangler's sides were heaving from the exhaustion of fighting the wind and snow that had brought her here. After a few minutes of rest, she nickered loudly, hoping someone would open the door and let her in out of the freezing cold wind. No one came. The door stayed shut. Tossing her head, she neighed again, then turned and kicked the door with her hind feet. That caused a ruckus inside the barn, and all the livestock started echoing their sentiments of having their sleep disrupted! Looking around in the shadowy night, the little filly saw the drifts around the buildings were not as deep as what she had come through to get to the ranch. A light came on in the house; it spread out of the windows and cast a glow over the snow on the front porch.

Wrangler walked over toward the house and was almost at the front step when the door opened and a figure stepped out with a lantern.

A tall rugged man held it up to see what the ruckus was about, for it had been loud enough he had heard it even with the wind blowing ninety to nothing.

At first Daniel didn't see anything but snow. Stepping further out onto the porch he saw a ghostly apparition of a horse and realized it was a little filly, snow packed into her coat. He couldn't figure out what she was doing out of the barn, but as he stepped closer, realized it wasn't one of his horses. As he held his hand out to her, Wrangler sniffed, tossed her head and wiggled her body like a wet dog. Clumps of snow fell off, revealing some of her sorrel color.

Just then the two children, Annabelle and William, stepped into the doorway, asking, "What is it, Pa?" They tried to peer around his tall, muscular frame. William stepped out beside his father, his eyes growing wide as he grabbed his father's hand, "Why it's Miss Rebecca's filly, what's she doing here?"

His father shook his head, "I have no idea, but the filly must have gotten out of her barn and drifted with the storm to the ranch. I'll put her in the barn for now, and you kids get back inside out of this wind." He turned and ushered the children in out of the night cold. They were in their pajamas, having left their beds to see what the noise was all about.

Putting on his heavy coat, mittens, and hat, Mr. Bonner picked up the lantern and told the children to head back to bed and that he would be back in just a few minutes. Walking out onto the front porch, he saw the little filly was standing patiently waiting for him. As he walked up to her, she turned and paused, as if waiting for him to lead.

"You're a pretty smart little thing, aren't you?" he said as he laid his hand on her snow-filled mane. Wrangler tossed her head as if to say, "Of course I am." That gesture brought a deep chuckle from him as he led her to the barn.

After feeding Wrangler some hay and grain, Daniel put a bucket of water in her stall. Using a stiff brush, he brushed out the clumps of snow that clung to her body hair. Then, lifting her small delicate hooves, he cleaned each one, removing the packed snow and ice. As he left the stall, she nickered softly and brushed her muzzle against his shoulder.

"Oh, are you saying thank you? Well now, you are very welcome, girl. I will see you in the morning to make sure you're doing alright." He closed the half gate and headed back to the warmth of the house, noticing the wind had died down and it was no longer snowing.

The children waited for him by the fireplace, jumping up when he entered the door.

"Pa, we have to go check on Miss Rebecca, something must have happened to her for her horse to come here!" William insisted, gazing up at his father with big pleading eyes.

"Yes, Poppa, we have to go check on Miss Rebecca," echoed Annabelle. Her worried tear-filled eyes were enough to twist anyone's heart, her father thought as he sat down at the table. She looked so much like her mother; it was almost more than he could bear sometimes.

"Well, I tell you what, I am sure that Miss Rebecca is just fine. Maybe the barn door wasn't latched against the wind and the horse just got out. This storm is almost over I think, and I will send one of the hands back with the filly to check on the teacher at daybreak."

"No, Pa. Wrangler is smart, she wouldn't leave Miss Rebecca alone unless something was wrong," William explained, pleading with his father. "She's more than just a horse, she knows tricks and everything! Miss Rebecca is wonderful with her; she trained her all by herself."

Hoping to help her brother, Annabelle grasped her father's hand, "Please, Poppa." A single tear escaped the corner of her eye to trickle down her cheek.

The angelic little face brought memories flooding into his heart and mind. His dear wife had passed away over four years ago, dying in childbirth. The doctor said there wasn't anything anyone could have done to change the outcome of that terrible night. But that hadn't helped him with the pain of losing her and the baby. There hadn't been any complications with the pregnancy until the last couple of months. Then his wife, Susan, had taken ill, losing her strength to do even the most menial of kitchen chores. When the labor started, it was over twenty hours of terrible pain that had finally drained her life away. Even the doctor was unsettled during the last few hours, knowing that the baby was already dead and the mother would not last much longer. He had taken care of the bodies and expressed to Daniel his heartfelt sorrow for the loss of Daniel's young wife and child. Doc knew it would be difficult enough in just losing his loved ones, but he now had two small children to raise on his own.

Shaking his head, Daniel cleared his thoughts of such sad memories and looked at his two dear children. It had taken him a long time to open up to them, and by the time he realized that, they had withdrawn into their own little worlds, hardly speaking at all.

They had grown thinner and were so quiet that he wondered why he had not noticed sooner. He had dealt with his own grief and hadn't seen what was right in front of him, he guessed. It had been about two years ago when he began coming back to the living and seeing how he had neglected the children's pain. Trying to make up for it, he had taken them to the school for lessons that his wife could no longer give them. He tried to spend time doing simple chores with them, reading aloud to them at bedtime and talking to them about their loss. At first they had only looked at him then walked away. But after a few weeks, their little hearts seemed to thaw. They had once again become his loving children, playful and talkative, except around other people. Then they were quiet and watchful, sometimes gazing off into the distance, lost in their own thoughts, shutting out the rest of the world.

Since the new schoolteacher had arrived, the children had opened up even more, telling their father all about school and what they were learning. He couldn't remember them ever talking about the old teacher at all, but they certainly talked about the "wonderful Miss Rebecca." He felt as if he knew her personally although he had not been to the schoolhouse since he had built the furniture and taken it there this last summer before the school year had started. The carpentry had helped him work his way through the sorrow by carving and working with wood. He was an excellent carpenter besides being a successful rancher.

Now that his children had almost recovered from the loss of their mother, his life was back to what some considered normal.

But there was something missing and he chose not to dwell on that. He would take care of the ranch and raise his son and daughter to be self-reliant because he loved them dearly. He wasn't sure he could ever love anyone again or even feel anything for another woman. Besides, he had enough to keep him busy with the children, the running of the ranch and the occasional piece of furniture he made in his spare time.

Coming out of his reverie, Daniel overheard his son telling his little sister that they could go back to the schoolhouse the next morning to check on Miss Rebecca. It would be just like going to school on any regular day, except that it was Christmas Eve. They would pack an extra lunch for her, too. Then she wouldn't have to be alone on Christmas Eve.

"Hey, now wait a minute, children, neither one of you is going out in this storm. If it breaks in the morning, I'll send a couple men to check on the teacher. I'm sure she is just fine and maybe she already has plans for company or is going somewhere for Christmas."

"Pa, it's a blizzard so she couldn't go anywhere, and besides, her horse is here now," William said. "And I heard the other kids ask her what she was doing for Christmas and she told them she was going to sew and read. So see, she doesn't have anyone to spend Christmas with. Now, she doesn't even have her horse," William said sadly. He gazed up at his father's face, willing him to understand what he was trying to say, that he didn't want her to be alone like they were without their mother.

Daniel watched the emotion flowing from his son's earnest face and slightly moist eyes. Then feeling a lump in his throat, he coughed and said, "Alright, in the morning I'll send someone to check on her."

"No Poppa," little Annabelle said as she glanced sideways at her brother. "Can't you go get her and bring her home for Christmas with us?"

"Well, she may not want to come back to the ranch if she has things that she wants to do there," he tried to explain to his young daughter.

"She would come if you went and asked her, I know she would. Please, Poppa? We'll be good and stay inside until you get back. Besides, Tex can stay with us while you're gone."

Tex was the ranch foreman who had been with Daniel since he first started the ranch. He was with the other hired hands just across the big yard in the bunkhouse weathering the storm. Tex loved the children as much as if they were his own kin, so he would be happy to watch out for them while the boss was gone.

Shaking his head, Daniel knew he would give in, so he said, "Alright, first thing in the morning, which is almost here, I'll saddle up a couple horses and go get Miss Rebecca, or I should say that I'll ask her if she wants to come here for Christmas."

With the last word barely leaving his mouth, his little girl flew into his arms! "Oh, Poppa! Thank you! She will be a wonderful Christmas gift!"

Hugging her tightly to him, he planted a kiss on the top of her head. Daniel looked at William, who stood gripping the edge of the table, a tear rolling down his freckled cheek. Holding out his other arm, Daniel drew him close and kissed his cheek, tasting the salty tear and realizing how much his children missed their mother. After a few moments, he ushered the children back to their beds, tucking them in and planting a kiss on each of their foreheads. Before he left their bedsides, he told each of them just how much he loved them. There was a time when he had forgotten to say those words and he regretted every day he hadn't. Daniel had vowed that not a day would go by without telling them.

Back in his empty room, he sighed, knowing it would be a short night as it was nearly morning already. He would need his rest for the morning's trip to fetch the "wonderful" Miss Rebecca to come back with him for Christmas. What had Annabelle called her? Oh yes, the Christmas gift.

CHAPTER 4

Rebecca had spent most of the day digging her way out. There was now a narrow path, just a little wider than her shoulders so she could turn back around and carry the snow to the far corner of the room. She kept the fire going, but not roaring as she didn't have a lot of wood, and there wasn't anything she was willing to burn at this point. As she worked, she recalled the last big storm back home in Maine that had blocked the doorway of the lighthouse. Her brothers had dug for hours, fashioning a tunnel from the house to the barn, cellar and outhouse. When they had finally broken through the first snowbank, it had been twenty feet high, and they couldn't even see the top of the barn. Only the top portion of the tall lighthouse was visible above the snow.

It was hours later in the day. Rebecca's arms were weak and she was bone tired. Having stopped and refilled the pans and pots with snow during her arduous labors, she now had plenty of drinking and bathing water on hand. But she was still unable to poke the broomstick through the snow and feel any give. Checking her little watch, she couldn't believe that it was after five o'clock in the afternoon.

Sighing heavily, she decided to eat something and rest for awhile. Rebecca unwrapped some of the homemade bread and put a small piece of cheese beside it on a little blue speckled tin plate. She still had a piece of prairie chicken one of the students had brought her the previous day, but she would keep it for tomorrow.

You just never knew how long a storm could last on the coast of Maine, and she really had no idea if it was the same in the Sandhills. Sipping her tea, she sat close to the small fire, looking forlornly at the meager pile of wood that was left. She could just kick herself for not bringing more in when she had been doing the chores! *Well, it was too late to cry over spilt milk now,* she thought. She would just have to let the fire die out for the night and restart it in the morning and pray it had stopped snowing and the chimney wasn't blocked.

Finishing off her tea and tidying up the table, she decided to read by the firelight before she went to bed. Later as she dressed for bed, she said a prayer that Wrangler would be alright and that she could dig out by morning and be able to get water and hay to the filly. It seemed she had no sooner snuggled down into the fluffy feather tick, than she closed her eyes and was fast asleep.

The winter storm continued through that night, but Rebecca was so tuckered out she never awoke once or heard the wind or the partial collapse of her tunnel.

The silence was what roused her from a deep dreamless sleep, not the cold. Opening her eyes, she saw the dim light cast meager shadows across the ceiling. She strained to hear any sound that might alert her to the tirade of the storm this morning. There was nothing. No howling wind, no screeching of wood rubbing against the roof or walls of the schoolhouse. The storm had stopped. Thank Heavens, she sighed.

Taking a bracing deep breath, Rebecca threw back the warm heavy covers, knowing the temperature in the room would be below the freezing point. Quickly she pulled on her petticoats, the heavy wool dress and warm winter boots. Shivering, she put together the makings of a small fire, hoping the chimney was not plugged with snow. The first match sputtered and went out. Shaking, she lit another one, having better luck. Carefully, she placed it on the dry moss, then blew softly to spread the flames. Laying a few small twigs on the flickering flames, she was able to feed in a couple of bigger sticks and finally added a good size piece of firewood.

Warmth was seeping into her as she filled the teakettle with snow and hung it above the flames on the fire hook. Even though she was anxious to have a cup of hot tea to warm her up, she knew it would take several minutes for the snow to melt and come to a boil.

Thankful that the chimney had not filled in with snow during the night, Rebecca watched the flames as they leaped upward, being drawn up the flue. Turning toward the door, she walked over, grabbed the bar and pushed it out of the locking piece and pulled on the door, holding her breath.

She cried out when she saw that the tunnel had partially collapsed, but she thought it seemed to look lighter toward the top now. She ran and grabbed her broom, shoving the handle upward as far as she could reach. There was a definite give this time! That meant she should be able to dig out if she went upwards. She could use the small stool in the corner to stand on, she thought as she hurried to get her basin and the stool. Standing on the stool was a little awkward, but she leaned against the door frame and started pulling the basin through the snow as high as she could reach. The snow seemed heavier than it did yesterday, she surmised. It must be from the collapsing of the tunnel. In only a few minutes her arms were weary with the reaching and pulling basin after basin of snow down into the room. She decided to take a little break, have some hot tea and then start again. She felt much warmer now, the fire having taken off the chill of the room and the labor having warmed her muscles.

Contemplating her next move, Rebecca figured she would be able to get through the snow in maybe the next round of digging at the top of the doorway if she could reach high enough. Making a cup of hot tea, she buttered a piece of bread, spread some jam on top and seated herself by the fire to enjoy her small repast.

Rebecca was swallowing the last of the tea when she thought she heard a noise outside. Hurrying to set down her teacup on the small table, she ran toward the door just as it burst open and a tall heavily-coated figure stepped in with snow following his path. A ray of sunlight shone from above, encircling the man as if he were an apparition.

Gasping in surprise, Rebecca wasn't sure if she was happy to see another person or not. Out here in the West not everyone was a welcome guest. Lost for words and because she couldn't see the man's face, she stepped backward toward the fireplace.

"Howdy, Ma'am," the tall man said as he took off the woolen scarf that encased his head and cowboy hat. Draping the wet scarf over the back of a chair, he then shut the door, pushing the snow out of the way with his large booted feet. Turning back toward her, he removed the heavy long bearskin coat and laid it over the extra chair.

When he raised his eyes and looked into her flashing green eyes, he stopped still. Neither one of them was able to voice what they thought or felt. It was like a bolt of lightning had struck them at the same time. He gazed at her, his hand halfway to his hat but going no further.

Rebecca had never seen anyone quite as tall as him before. His shoulders were wide, narrowing into a muscular but lean chest and arms. His size was intimidating, but she knew immediately that he wouldn't hurt her. She tried to clear her throat, struggling to say something, but unable to utter a sound. She dreamily stepped forward, raising a hand toward him, intending to welcome him. At the same instant, the tall cowboy stepped closer to her, taking her hand in his, never breaking their intense gaze.

As a soft charming smile slowly spread across his face, the cowboy said, "You must be the infamous Miss Rebecca that my children have talked about."

Catching her breath once again, Rebecca relaxed and smiled back, still wondering who this tall cowboy could be. "Yes, I am the schoolteacher, Miss Rebecca. And who might you be, sir?"

At this, the cowboy laughed lightly and said, "I'm Daniel Bonner. Annabelle and William are my children, and the reason I am here to rescue you from the storm."

Realizing that he was still holding her hand in his, Rebecca drew it swiftly back, feeling ridiculous for having such strange thoughts about this man. Besides he was the father of two of her students. She felt a very strong attraction to this good-looking man, but she would have to quell those feelings, knowing who he was.

"Oh, I appreciate your concern, sir, but I don't need rescuing," Rebecca laughed lightly. "Besides I was almost dug out. I was going to go check on my horse in the barn and bring in more firewood and food supplies from the storm cellar."

"Well, I hate to tell you, but half of your little shed is gone, and your horse is over at my place," he said, relinquishing her hand as she stepped back over to the fire.

"What? Is she alright? How far do you live from here? I'll come get her as soon as I get dressed properly," Rebecca stated, starting to gather up her heavy coat and mittens.

"Now hold on, ma'am. She is just fine in my barn for the time being and it's a little too far for you to consider walking all the way. It's a ways past the ridge west of here, about three miles, I'd say. And with all this snow and drifting, I don't think you'd make it on your own."

Rebecca mumbled something unintelligible under her breath, rebelling against someone telling her what she was capable of or not!

Seeing the color come up in Rebecca's cheeks, Daniel had a pretty good idea that she was a little bit stubborn when it came to being told she couldn't do something and would fight tooth and nail till she did it. That thought made him laugh out loud.

Lifting her chin up in defiance, Rebecca protested, "I can walk that far, you don't need to laugh at me!"

"I'm not laughing at you, it's just your feisty attitude!"

"I am most certainly capable of walking to your place. I have warm enough wraps to protect me. I just need to know what direction and what landmarks to look for."

"Now look, Miss Rebecca, I know you are mighty independent from what my children have told me, but they did send me to fetch you back to our house for Christmas.

"Christmas?" Oh heavens, I simply forgot today is Christmas Eve! You should be home with your family, not here. I can take care of myself, but thank you all the same!"

"Well, I hate to tell you but I'm not going back without you. I can't go back without you…the children are expecting you as kind of their Christmas gift."

"What do you mean? Their Christmas gift?"

"Cause that's what they said they wanted for Christmas, for me to bring you back to the ranch, so you would be safe and not alone on Christmas. I don't think that you would want to disappoint two small children now, would you?" Daniel said, smiling teasingly at Rebecca, but using her regard for the children to his advantage.

"Oh, but I really can't impose on you at Christmas time," Rebecca said, but was thinking of how much more she would like to get to know this man. A man who had come to "rescue" her for his children's sake.

"It's alright, besides, you don't have a place to keep your horse now, so you can stay at the ranch a few days while I send over some men to fix the little shed," Daniel said, knowing that he probably sounded pushy, but did not want to take no for an answer. And not just because of his children! He really wanted to spend more time with this "Miss Rebecca."

"I am just fine here at the school, really," Rebecca said, although she felt a pang at having forgotten that today was even Christmas Eve and she was alone. Alright, she wasn't alone right this minute, but he would be leaving soon and then she would be. Alone. For Christmas. All by herself. But wasn't that what she had planned?

"There is no reason that you can't come and spend a few days till the weather warms up, and I'll bring you back safe and sound," Daniel stated, knowing he didn't want to disappoint his children. And he was still feeling the sensation he had felt when he had first laid eyes on her. Like he had to be near her.

This is nonsense, Rebecca thought, remembering when he had first appeared through the doorway. Still feeling the tingling feeling pulsing through her, she picked up the teakettle, turning toward the fireplace. "Would you like a cup of warm tea before you head back to your ranch?"

"Boy Howdy! You are stubborn!" Daniel said as he stepped toward the fireplace, stopping directly behind her. Reaching over her shoulder, he removed the tea kettle from her hand and hung it back on the hook over the fire.

Startled, Rebecca unconsciously stepped backward, coming abruptly to a stop up against a rock-hard body. Her heart pounded as she felt his hands on her shoulders turning her around to face him. Gazing up at him, she couldn't think of a thing to say in response to the naked look of yearning in his dark brown eyes, but her body reacted naturally, willing her to respond even though she knew she shouldn't. He was a man with two small children, her students, for Heaven's sake!

Daniel was unable to resist the urge to taste Rebecca's succulent lips. Bending his head, he took them in a kiss that ignited him and Rebecca. Then, just as suddenly, he set her away from him, staring at the lips that beckoned him still.

Breaking the spell, Rebecca stepped sideways away from Daniel, sucking in air like she didn't know what it was. What was happening to her? She hadn't ever felt this way before. She actually wanted him to touch her, hold her, to kiss her even! Heavens! There was no way she could go to his ranch and stay. It would be too difficult. Too dangerous!

Daniel sat down on a chair, shaking his head while looking at Rebecca's back, and then slowly he took all of her in. The long auburn hair pulled back in a braid and tied with a ribbon. It was almost the same color as her little sorrel filly, Wrangler, that the children were so impressed with. Whatever had made him kiss her, had hit him hard.

Her defiant stance was immobile for a few moments, when she suddenly spun around and stated, "I'm sorry but I really can't go home with you. I will be just fine here. Please tell the children that I will see them when school starts up again in a couple weeks."

Rising to tower over her, Daniel began, "Now, listen Miss Rebecca, I am not leaving here without you. I will not disappoint my children on Christmas Eve! So if you don't want to be hog tied, flung over my saddle and hauled back to the ranch like a pig in a poke, you had better be packing a bag and getting ready to go! Got it, sister?" Daniel was amazed that he had spoken to this woman like that, but was positive he wouldn't win the decision any other way.

Rebecca was astonished that this man would talk to her this way. She started to sass him then thought better of it for in her heart she didn't want to disappoint the children, she felt compelled to give them what they desired. "Alright but I am only doing this for your children! Not for you!" Or at least that's what she told herself. Whirling around, she went to her bed and pulled a small carpetbag from underneath, opened it up and went to the carved wooden chest, running her hand over the beautiful work before pulling out some clothing and placing it in the bag.

Daniel Bonner watched Rebecca as she packed her bag, not missing how she touched the furniture he had lovingly carved. She liked it, and he knew she appreciated the craftsmanship by the way she touched the scrolling on the corners and the hand-carved wooden handles. A sense of pride rose up to cause a slight lump in his throat. Here was a good woman. He knew she was kind and caring, from what the children had told him about her. And he had just seen for himself that she could be very stubborn and independent. He had reacted to the fire in her green eyes when she was being contrary, feeling the heat rise in his loins when she had backed into him accidently. Hell, from the first second he had laid eyes on her, he was entrapped. Now what to do about it would be a real corker!

Coming out of his reverie, Daniel noticed that she was finished and pulling on her heavy woolen coat and a woolen cap over her hair, letting the braid hang down her back. The shining auburn braid reached just past her waistline, making him wonder what it would look like all loose and flowing on his pillow. Hmm, that would be interesting, he mused.

Rebecca spoke again. Apparently the man was hard of hearing, she thought, peering up at him intently. Why, he seemed to not be here at all, except for the small smile lifting the corners of his mouth. She was curious about what he was thinking, but instead repeated her words, "I'm ready to go, Mr. Bonner."

"Oh, right, I will go out first and pull you up onto the top of the drift. It won't be too hard, just do not let go of my hand, okay? Daniel climbed up the snowdrift, kicking his boots into the snow, making a stairway up and out from the schoolhouse door. Once on top, he told her to hand up her bag, then he reached back down for her mittened hands. Rebecca started to slip and made a little squeal, but Daniel pulled her easily the rest of the way out of the little tunnel to the top of the huge snowdrift that covered the side of the schoolhouse. The sun was reflected on the new fallen snow, but clouds were slowly drifting south across the sky giving relief to the brightness.

Rebecca was amazed at the transformed landscape around her. The little shed that had housed her filly now appeared to be only a few boards poking through the snow. She was relieved that Wrangler had escaped any injuries and had found shelter at the Bonner Ranch. *Would she?*

By the corral fence, there stood a couple of saddle horses waiting patiently for them as they slid down the huge snow drift and walked across a barren patch of ground. Rebecca turned and looked up at the handsome rancher. "How can there be a drift that blocks in the whole schoolhouse and crushes the shed, then here is open uncovered ground?"

"When the wind gets going in a blizzard, you would be surprised at what it can do out here in the Sandhills," Daniel replied as he tied her bag to the saddle horn and turned to help her mount up. It was a little awkward for her to mount with all the heavy clothing and cumbersome coat. She wasn't able to sit in the saddle properly, so Daniel deftly lifted her back off the horse and set her down on the ground. "Here, let me fix your coat," and pulling out a long hunting knife from the inside of his heavy winter boot, he sliced down the back seam, adapting her long winter coat like his own heavy bearskin coat. It allowed her to sit in the saddle, covering the front and sides of her legs and parting to cover her backside without bunching up on the saddle. Just as quickly, he lifted her back into the saddle, surprising her with his strength, that he could lift her so easily with all the clothes and the heavy coat she was wearing as if she weighed nothing. Not admitting to herself the little thrill that it gave her.

Daniel handed up the reins to her horse then mounted his own, leading the way to his ranch. With the amount of meandering it would take to bypass all the deep snow and huge drifts, it would take about two hours to reach the ranch. The sun was already warming the air. It wasn't melting the snow, but it was definitely warmer than yesterday, he thought as they rode out.

Rebecca pondered over her strange feelings for this rugged man that rode in front of her, leading her through drifts up to the bellies of the horses sometimes and then over clear patches of dry grass and sand. It was the strangest thing, she thought, her odd reaction to this man. But she was curious about him. She knew there could never be anything between them because he was the father of two of her students. So stop it! She told herself. Think of the children and seeing them. She would be able to see what their home life was like and maybe draw them come out of their shells even more. She couldn't help but look forward to that. The way that Mr. Bonner had talked about their pleading for him to come fetch her, they had sounded like two different children than the ones she knew at school. Maybe they were more talkative at home. That's probably right; some children were like that she knew from watching other parents with their children at school.

On the way back to the Bonner Ranch, Daniel explained what had happened with his wife and the children. He wasn't sure why, but he felt she needed to know more about him and his family. In turn, Rebecca told him about her parents and brothers back in Maine and how she felt she was meant to be here in the Sandhills teaching. They fell into easy conversation the rest of the way and before she realized it, they rode into the ranch yard in front of a large ranch house. Rebecca felt like she had known Daniel for years instead of a few hours.

As they pulled up their horses, a young cowboy stepped out from the front door and took the reins of their horses as Daniel dismounted. Daniel stepped over to Rebecca's mount and easily lifted her from her saddle. The physical attraction was growing between them. Rebecca could hardly take her eyes off him as Daniel set her down, and he didn't stop gazing into hers either.

Daniel had to force himself to let go of her and not drag her up against him for a kiss that he knew would be shattering. He kept thinking of her hair loose, running his hands through it, pulling her to him. *Wanting her.* That thought was suddenly interrupted by Tex.

"Well, hello, Boss." The young man said, turning to Rebecca with a grin as wide as Texas, "You have got to be Miss Rebecca, the kids have been talking all morning about you."

"Tex, this is Miss Rebecca, the school teacher," Daniel said, looking back to Rebecca.

Rebecca colored as the cowboy openly appraised her. She thought he probably would be lovesick at the sight of any young woman though, out here where they were few and far between. Even though she was flattered, she caught a glimpse of Mr. Bonner's face and could see that he seemed a little irritated. But why should he care if a cowboy looked at her that way? "Pleased to meet you, Tex."

Just then the two children came running out of the house, almost knocking her off her feet as they hugged her. Both were chattering and smiling, tugging her up the steps into the ranch house. Daniel smiled as he followed them all inside, watching the joy on his children's faces for the first time in a really long while. He was glad he had given in to his children and fetched Miss Rebecca to the ranch. Life certainly was looking a lot more interesting.

Rebecca waited for a housekeeper to appear, but no one came. The children helped her off with her coat, and Mr. Bonner took her bag and heavy boots to set them on a bench along the wall. He left the room, so she figured he would bring back the housekeeper or whoever helped take care of his children and the house.

In a few minutes, Daniel came back into the room, warming his hands at the fireplace where Rebecca sat in a hand-carved rocking chair. Neither said anything, but they both drank in the sight of each other, knowing there was something growing between them.

"I laid out some food in the kitchen as I imagine you are probably about starved. I even have some tea brewing," Daniel said, knowing from their conversation during the ride that she loved her tea.

The children were already seated and waiting for them in the kitchen. Everyone was hungry but talked about Christmas, the blizzard and the tricks that Wrangler was able to do. After finishing lunch, the children cleared the dishes and helped Daniel and Rebecca wash and dry. It felt strange, but wonderful all at the same time, Rebecca thought, as she hung up her towel and followed Daniel into the living room. Daniel seated her in the rocker, and he sat on a dark leather chair facing her, both basking in the heat of the fireplace. The children had run down the hall a few minutes ago and all was quiet.

As she warmed herself by the big fireplace, the children returned bringing a book and asked their father to read to them. The book was about the birth of Christ and how Christmas came to be. The children leaned against her chair with a blanket wrapped around them. As she watched Daniel read to his children, her heart was full. What a good father he was, she thought. He would be a good husband, too. Now where did that thought come from? But she just couldn't help herself, it was true, she just knew he was a good man.

At the end of the story, the children brought a blanket to cover her lap, then raced out of the room. Watching them, Rebecca laughed and was thankful she had given in and come to the ranch for Christmas. She enjoyed being with Daniel and the children. Squealing with delight, William and Annabelle ran around the house putting up some popcorn stringers they had made the night before with red ribbons for decoration. They were definitely caught up in the excitement of Christmas!

After finishing the decorating, the children seemed to be calmer now, but looked like they had a secret. They kept glancing at each other and then the door…what was going on, Rebecca thought. The two ran out of the room, giggling to themselves. What were they up to?

When Daniel returned to the living room, Rebecca stood up and stepped toward him, meeting him at the doorway. She half expected to see someone come with him. But he was alone.

"Do you and the children live here alone?"

"Yes, we do, why?" Daniel answered.

"Oh, I thought you would have a housekeeper."

"We do, but she doesn't live with us. Her family lives and works on the ranch. She is spending the holidays with her family."

"Then who is staying with you and the children?" Rebecca almost squeaked.

"Why you are, Miss Rebecca." Daniel said as he smiled at her, watching the color rise in her cheeks.

"Oh!" Rebecca trailed off, not knowing what to say next. But she had this feeling of excitement at having him and his children all to herself and she couldn't explain why. She thought of the children and how different they were here at home, outgoing and chattering like the other children at school. It was clear that they loved their father and maybe that made it easier when he was around. And it was obvious that Mr. Bonner loved his children, look at what he had done to get her here! Her emotions flooded her heart and mind, thinking how Mother Nature had definitely taken a hand in their meeting this way.

She remembered her mother always telling the story of how she had met Rebecca's father and how it had been love at first sight! But she had always thought it was just that. A story! Now thinking of her sudden unbidden reaction to Daniel Bonner, she wondered if it just might be true?

At that moment, a pair of squealing children holding a long stick with something tied in a bright red ribbon swung it over their teacher's head and hollered, "Kiss the teacher, Papa. You have to kiss the Christmas gift!"

Looking up, Rebecca now recognized what the little bundle was. Mistletoe. An impish grin spreading across her face, Rebecca looked at William and Annabelle, seeing the delight in their young faces and thought how easy it would be to love these children. Looking up at Daniel, she thought, *and oh how easy it would be to love this man!*

Daniel smiled down at her and his two darling children, thanking God and Mother Nature for the storm that had brought Rebecca to them. "Yes, I suppose I must! Pulling Rebecca into his arms, he murmured, "Come here, Christmas Gift!" as he lowered his lips to hers.

Starstruck

By

LK Lien

Chapter 1

Molly used to love Christmas. Not anymore.

Being alone at that time of year meant forcing smiles during other people's Christmases. Of course people asked her to their homes. Kind, loving invites. Or even worse, pity invites.

Some people got to work during Christmas. The newspaper came out every day, after all. She had volunteered. She needed to have a reason to stay away from other people's celebrations. Her brother wouldn't believe any other excuse but work. His wife, however, would jump on any excuse not to have Molly intruding on their family holiday.

The managing editor had kindly but firmly told her that there was no need for the science editor to work at Christmas. Bah humbug!

Light flashed across the newsroom. Somebody had plugged in the Christmas tree. A bright blue aluminum tree with silver lights and silvery ornaments that drank in the room light and splashed it out a hundredfold.

Okay. She still loved this holiday, the lights and music. The way people treated one another. Secret Santas. She turned to shut off her computer. Time to go. Less than a week until Christmas. Gifts to find. Gifts to wrap. Cookies to bake. Her spirits lifted.

A NASA alert flashed into her inbox. She cancelled her computer shutdown, intrigued. NASA sent several newsflashes a day. She filed about half into the future files, possible stories for someday. The other half she trashed. But this one fairly screamed "urgent."

A bright new star had appeared in the sky.

Chapter 2

Molly was hot and tired and thirsty and hungry, shaky after being on a plane for 15 hours. And thrilled to the tips of her toes. Three days ago she'd been in the newsroom in Des Moines, Iowa. Now she was heading to the Australian Outback, following a star.

Her ears perked up as the announcement to board the connecting flight came over the speakers. Her heart scampered outside where people were boarding the little plane sitting on the tarmac. Her suitcase-laden body, alas, remained inside the Sydney terminal, moving in slow motion through the crowds. The place was packed. Journalists, scientists and excited tourists and their kids -- screaming, running, out-of-control kids -- had flocked to Australia to see the star. People couldn't see it from the north. Certainly not from Iowa. This star shined only in the southern skies. You could see it from southern Texas and Mexico, from Florida. But to really see it in all its glory, you had to come to Ayers Rock, deep inside Australia.

Molly eyed the railing of the shaky, flimsy portable stairs leading up to the small plane. Not as small as a Cessna or anything, but still. Not exactly confidence-boosting. Flying sent the bad side of her imagination soaring. But even a small puddle-jumper flight was worth it to get to come on this journey. The shiny new star was a bonus. Or really, Australia was the bonus. The star was the main attraction. She didn't care. She was excited about it all, the whole package. She'd always dreamed of visiting the Australian

Outback. And now, there was the star too, 5 million times as bright as our sun. Even 7,500 light-years away, it was the brightest thing in the night sky.

She looked up. Stopped in her tracks. Chided herself for her silliness. Stars don't come out in the day. But there it was. Shining in the daylit sky alongside the sun. What the...? She was dumbstruck. Awestruck. Struck from behind. Hurled into space. Hey!

A tanned muscular arm enveloped her, halting her forward motion mid-fall. "Sorry about that. Didn't expect the whole coming to a screeching halt thing."

"Maybe you shouldn't have been following so close. Unhand me, varlet."

A snort behind her, the steel-in-velvet arm disappearing as suddenly as it had appeared. "I live to serve, milady."

She looked around, and up. At 5'9", she was pretty tall for a woman, but the man rose above her like a stone pillar. A cute, rugged-looking pillar with glasses and sun-streaked brown hair, vivid blue eyes and a friendly grin that grew appreciatively wider as he caught sight of her face.

"Um..."

His smile widened. "Couldn't have put it better myself."

A blush betrayed her. Damn. She moved away.

"What o'ertook you, milady, that you came to such a sudden halt?"

She let out a distinctly unladylike snort of her own. He made her want to laugh. She stiffened her spine, looking for a distraction from this charmer. Charm usually hid snakes. Snaky charmer.

She looked up, toward the skies this time, wonder overpowering practical skepticism. "That's the star. Eta Carinae. In the middle of the day. I mean, I knew it was bright, but it's out in the day. No one told me you could see it in the day."

"Amazing, isn't it? Of course, it's not one star, it's a binary system. Two stars together."

"Hey, Bud, don't rain on my parade. It looks like one star. It's amazing. Let me stop and smell the starshine."

"Smelly starshine it is." He gestured towards the plane. "They're waiting for us. We're the last ones." He reached down, pulling one of her suitcases away.

"Hey! What are you doing?"

"You look a little overladen there. Just lightening your burden."

"Ask first. I've got it, thanks." She jerked her suitcase back. The starstruck, manstruck bubble popped. She hated it when men just took over. She headed towards the stairs, trying to balance the luggage while still gripping the flimsy railing, and tripped.

"You better not be laughing," she said not quite under her breath enough, wobbling up the stairs, facing firmly in front.

"Never crossed my mind," she heard behind her, laughter manfully restrained. Then not.

The muscular arm reached in front of her again, carefully not touching her. He gave a little tug on the suitcase in her right arm. "Let me help. Already ran into you once today. And hey, if we wait until you teeter up these stairs with your arms full, the star will have burned out by the time we get on the plane."

"Thanks," muttered ungraciously.

"My pleasure, milady." The laughter in the voice again. He really was cute. Too bad he was so full of himself.

* * *

No overhead bins in this small plane. She paused before the front luggage closet, reaching behind to take back her luggage. She didn't trust her camera and binoculars to anyone. He widened his eyes in false affront, but gave up her luggage without comment. Without verbal comment anyway. Laughter still filled his face. He gave a sweeping bow, indicating she should go ahead of him into the plane.

As soon as she crossed through the plane door, the noise level reached out and smacked her. Confused, she stopped abruptly.

"Whoa!" The laughing male voice behind her yet again. "What is it this time? Another star?"

She huffed, tossing her long auburn hair so it swatted him, grabbed the first empty seat. The kid right behind her kicked her seat, letting out a wail. Her irritating rescuer's grin deepened.

She heard him excusing himself as he passed other passengers, then heard a strident female voice. "Have you been saved? The star is coming to bring home the saved. Here, let me read this pamphlet to you."

She looked back. He was trapped in the last available seat by a rough-looking woman on a mission. A grin spread across her own face. He glared at her. She gave him a little finger wave, smiling even wider.

Chapter 3

"Do you need a guide, Lady? I can tell you all about this star. My people know all about her."

Molly looked down at the Aboriginal kid standing near Ayers Rock and sparkling with enthusiasm. "Her?"

"Yes! This star is the wife of Crow. A pretty lady like you would like to know about this pretty star, right? I've lived here all my life. I know all the stories of my people. I can make you a good deal."

Oh man, another charmer. What was it with gallant males in this country?

"All your life, huh? What's that? 10?"

"11," he said with affronted dignity. "11 in 5 weeks."

"I don't know, kid. I need to talk to some of the leaders around here. I need to find out what people think about this star appearing. Whether it's seen as important or not. Whether they think Christmas has anything to do with it. And I guess now I need to find out about Mrs. Crow."

"Lady, I can tell you all about that star. I already told you she's the wife of Crow, right? See, you didn't even know that. I can introduce you to the oldest people of my family, if that's what you want. My grandfather is 89."

"Is he really?" Molly looked at the kid speculatively. "Okay. I tell you what. We'll try it for a while and see how it goes.

Charge me a fair rate and I'll throw in a bonus in the end. Or my newspaper will, anyway. And I mean, fair to you too."

The boy lit up. "You have a deal, Lady. You won't be sorry. I'm the best guide around."

Molly held back a smile. The truth was, this kid seemed like a sweetie, and he did appear to know his stuff. He was also just about the only game in town. The place was swarming with media stars who'd gotten here earlier. They'd already snatched up the university professors, astronomers and geologists who could explain the science of the star in the sky and the science of Ayers Rock. They'd also snatched up the Aboriginal leaders. Of course the professors and elders would rather talk to National Geographic or CBS News than the Des Moines Register. She didn't want to duplicate everyone else's stories anyway.

"Okay, kid. You've got a deal. I'm Molly Larsen. What's your name?"

"Daku. You won't be sorry. You don't want to waste time. Where do you want to go first?"

Molly laughed. The kid's enthusiasm was catching, not that she wasn't already enthused to the max. "First off, tell me something about Ayers Rock. Sorry. You call it Uluru, right?"

"Uluru. Yes. It's sacred to our people. I can guide you around it."

"Can we climb it?"

Daku frowned. "People do climb it. It's not forbidden. But our people don't do it. It's not respectful. I can help you figure out how to get up there though, if you really want."

"No. That's okay. I don't want to be disrespectful. And you go ahead and tell me if I'm doing something to offend people. That's partly why I'm hiring you, so you can guide me through the customs here too.

Daku's wild enthusiasm bounced back. "Okay, Lady. Molly. Let's go."

* * *

Uluru was incredible, a giant glowy monolith in the middle of nowhere. Molly could absolutely understand why it was a sacred site. Right here, it felt like a miracle was teetering on the edge of happening, or maybe, already underway.
An amazing coincidence, if that's what it was, a new star appearing right at Christmas, seeming to shine the brightest here, at this even more ancient sacred site. That was what she'd written about in her first story. She hadn't intended to write about "the Christmas miracle." The star had only appeared three days ago, and she was already tired of that theme. Every reporter on the planet had grabbed that idea and run with it.

But here, she couldn't help herself. Wonder seemed to flow out like some sacred radiation. She stretched out, basking in the happy glow. And was clunked on the head.

"What the…? Ow!" She straightened up rapidly, instinctively reaching to grab the shiny metal object as it bounced off her head. Overhead, a crow cried out, its raspy call laughing at her as it circled overhead.

Daku bounced over, waving at the crazy bird. "What did he drop?"

"I don't know." Molly stared down at her hand still closed around the object. "But ow! You should be asking if I'm injured. I'm lucky I'm not dead."

Daku shot her a look of disbelief. "You're standing up and talking. How bad can it be? Besides, this is lucky. Crow has honored you."

"Funny way of showing it. He just bopped me on the head. Hard."

Daku grinned. "Crow never gives gifts straight. He likes to cause trouble. What do you suppose his gift will be? He's the husband of this star, remember. If Crow is appearing now, it has to be special. This is awesome! Your life is going to change."

"What if I don't want my life to change?" Molly argued. "I'm happy with the way things are. This Crow can't just go around changing things without asking people."

"Uh, yes, he can. Don't worry. You're honored. You'll like the changes even better. Probably." He gave a little hop. "So, come on, what did he drop on you? Don't you want to see?"

Molly opened up her fist, staring. "It's a flashdrive."

Daku craned over her hand. "Wow! I wonder what's on it!"

"Do you think it still works? It was just dropped from the sky."

"Well, come on! Put it in your laptop and see what's on it!"

Molly looked at him, a little startled that she hadn't thought of that right away. But she had just been hit on the head after all.

Chapter 4

Molly and Daku gasped in delight as picture after picture flowed across her laptop screen, each more spectacular than the last, showing the star in all its glory.

"Oooh!"

"Sweet!"

"This is exactly what I need for my articles. I wonder who this drive belongs to."

"Crow must want you to use those pictures or he wouldn't have given you this drive."

"Come on. Would Crow even know what a flashdrive is?"

Daku looked at her with exasperation. "He's a god being from the Dreamtime. Of course he knows about computers. He can get into our minds."

"Yuck. I don't want some mischievous trickster god-thing rooting around in my mind."

"Oh grow up," Daku said, grinning suddenly as she stared at him in mock outrage, well partly mock anyway. He giggled. "Well, what do you think gods and spirits do, anyway? It doesn't matter what you want. It matters what the god-people want.

"This star is Crow's Wife, and look…" He leaned forward, pointing at the onscreen photo. "These little stars around Crow's Wife are their children. You think he's not going to pay attention to everything about his star wife? This is all about him and his family."

"Well, not all about him and his family. The star just happened to burst out right at Christmas, remember. Another star was awfully important 2,000 years ago too. Maybe this star has to do with that child. Or maybe it's all just coincidence."

"But everything is connected. That's what Dreamtime is. You Americans always want things to fit into neat, separate little compartments. The world is like water. Everything mixes together. How can you not see that?"

Molly looked at Daku. "You're rather awesome yourself, you know. "

"I do know." He sparkled with joyful laughter, his seriousness forgotten.

Molly regarded him with great affection. He really was most charming and sweet. Maybe not all charm was bad. At least not in a 10-year-old kid.

"Hey!"

A shadow darkened Molly and Daku as they crouched down over the laptop. They looked up, and up. An angry man loomed over them.

"What are you doing with my photos? Is that my flashdrive? What the heck!?!"

Molly stared in amazement. It was the oh-so-charming guy from the plane. Only not so charming now. She stood up slowly, putting herself between the man and Daku.

"Oh, you again."

He glared.

"Well, we were looking at these photos, if they are yours, which I doubt. I don't know if it's your flashdrive or not. How did you lose it?"

"How did you get it?"

"How did you lose it? I asked you first."

His lips tightened over clenched teeth.

Daku said, "Hey, I thought I was the kid."

Molly blushed, but refused to back down.

"You first. I want to know how you lost the flashdrive."

"Okay. You won't believe it, I'm warning you, but I'd just taken it out of my laptop when this giant, crazy crow swooped down from the sky, divebombing me. Its claws were outstretched, and I thought it was going to tear into my face, like 'The Birds' or something."

Daku and Molly exchanged glances, their heads swiveling back to catch the rest of the story.

"I know it sounds crazy…"

"Not as crazy as you might think," Molly said dryly. Daku bounced with excitement.

"Is that so? Why not? Tell me how you found the drive," her nemesis demanded.

"I'll tell you ours when you finish telling yours."

The man shot her a skeptical look. "Okay. That's about it. When this crazy crow divebombed me, I dropped the drive and rolled back. The crow grabbed the flashdrive in midair and flew off with it before I could catch it. The end. Your turn."

"Do you see this?" Molly pointed to the lump on her forehead.

"Yeah. That looks painful. What happened anyway? Are you okay? What's that got to do with my flashdrive?"

"Your crow"

"Not *my* crow"

"Dropped *your* flashdrive on *my* head! From the sky!"

He stared at her incredulously, then began to laugh.

The muscles in Molly's face tightened ferociously. Her eyes compressed into slivers. He laughed even harder.

She tried to keep glaring, but, okay, it was a little bit funny. His laughter was contagious. She stopped fighting it.

Chapter 5

Mark, Molly and Daku, The Team of Crow, as the three had started calling themselves, sat under an awning, grateful for any shade in the 100-degree heat, making little sounds of pleasure as the cool, pearly gelato slid into their mouths. Enterprising vendors had set up food trucks everywhere, taking advantage of the recent burst of star-tourists.

Even better, Mark and Molly had finally gotten around to introducing themselves. Not something she would have expected to cause her any happiness. One more unexpected pleasure this Christmas.

"Weirdest Christmas I've ever had," she said.

"I was just thinking that too," Mark agreed. "But, weird in a good way." He smiled at her warmly.

Oh, boy, Molly thought, fighting to control the shiver arising from the wild mix of joy, anticipation, fear Mark's smile caused her.

"How is it weird?" Daku asked.

"Well, for one thing," Mark answered, "It's hot as heck here. It's winter in America now. In Colorado, where I live, it's cold and snowy now."

"Yeah, in Iowa too," Molly agreed.

"I've never seen snow," Daku said. "I've seen pictures on the Internet though."

"Well, maybe we'll figure out a way to get you to come visit and play in our snow," Molly said.

Daku's grin nearly exploded across his face.

"And of course," Mark continued, "there's this star. That is definitely weird."

"Not to mention a mad Crow bomber you say is a god being."

"Very weird."

"Unexpected, at the very least."

Daku regarded them carefully. "Are you sure you two didn't know each other in America? It seems like you fit together."

Molly felt herself blush, hating the way her body seemed to have developed a mind of its own.

"No, we've never met. But I would like to make up for lost time," Mark said, turning to look at Molly. Again.

Warm pink washed over her face. Again. Damn. Damn. The traitorous coloring made her furious with herself.

"I'm here to work," she said sharply. Mark and Daku looked at her in surprise. "I'm sorry. It's just, I probably only have a few more days here, and this story is important. I need to concentrate on work. I'm not here to play."

"Well, I'm here to work too," Mark said mildly. "I play during the day, work during the night."

Molly snatched at this opening in relief. "Don't people usually play at night?" Oh hell. That's not how she meant it to sound. Watching the delighted mischief spread across Mark's face,

Molly tried to smother the uncontrollable blush hijacking her body again. "I meant. What do you do at night?"

His Hugh Jackman grin spread even wider.

She threw up her hands, forced each word out, one by one. "What work do you do at night?"

He took pity, a little anyway. He was still grinning that cat grin. "I'm an astronomer."

Molly perked up. She switched to work mode. Really. "I don't suppose you'd let me interview you, would you? And use your pictures for the stories?"

She'd already asked to buy his photos for the paper. He'd suggested they all talk about it over gelato. And here they were. They'd strayed from business quickly, talking easily about everything and nothing. Daku was right, she thought. It was as if she and Mark had known each other for years. And Daku fit right in too.

It was a blessing Daku was there, in more ways than one. The presence of a kid served to damp down the annoyingly distracting desire that seemed to be bubbling up throughout her body. She couldn't believe this was happening now. She had work to do. And she didn't trust a man with so much charm.

Her last boyfriend, Tom, had been full of charm, and she'd fallen for him like a ton of bricks. About two years ago, he'd left her abruptly, moving out of their house, telling her he'd never planned on anything permanent with her, noting calmly that he'd always known he could do better than her. The charm had all been fake. He was just as charming as he'd needed to be.

Of course, looking back now, she could see the signs. The charm had been calculated, but she'd been too naïve, she'd been too in love, wanted the relationship too much, to see the warnings.

But now, in spite of Mark's charm, she wasn't seeing any signs he was that full of himself. In fact, he seemed amazingly decent. He'd certainly been kind and playful with Daku, including him naturally in their Team of Crow. The way people treated the powerless said everything.

But still. She could be in a lot of trouble with this sexy, charming, kind, intelligent man. She didn't have room for this, this, distraction, in her life. She didn't know if she was strong enough to take another rejection. Not that it had even gotten to the rejection point yet. It hadn't even gotten to the dating part yet, who was she kidding, although it did seem as if he were making moves in that direction. She just couldn't afford to take the risk.

And yet. Her awakened feelings were painful and sharp, exciting and glorious, all rolled together. Being with this man was intoxicating. She got hold of herself. She had to be firm. She didn't want a little Australian affair. She wanted something lasting. This Christmas adventure would be over in a few days. Best to keep it professional. She girded her loins.

Chapter 6

Molly was preparing to write her next story, centered around the science of the Christmas star, as explained by University of Denver astrophysics professor Mark Kirkpatrick. It would be a perfect companion piece to the one she'd written about the mystical connections to this bright shining star. Mark had been perfect, explaining everything in clear, scientific terms. His pictures were perfect too. And she wanted to smack him.

After talking with her and Daku, he'd gone online to read her previous stories about the star. And he'd laughed at them. Not out loud. It was worse than that. He'd been condescending. Polite and dismissive.

She'd written about the ancient legends of Crow, tying them into the fact that the Aborigines thought this bright, glorious star was his wife. And tying the tales of Crow to a more recent story, about wise men following a star.

He couldn't quite keep his dismissal hidden. She hadn't been trying to convince anyone the legends were true. She didn't believe it was Mrs. Crow up there. But still. The stories were all about wonder and magic and miracles. And she did believe in them.

Arrogant pig. How could somebody who could talk so eloquently about the marvels of the universe fail to see that he *was* talking about miracles and wonders. Mysteries.

That was the real mystery. How somebody so smart could be so…dumb. And how she could be so dumb as to fall for this…man.

Daku was deep into hero worship. Mark hadn't been patronizing with the kid. He'd listened to Daku seriously, respectfully. That wasn't how he'd treated her. He'd made no secret of the fact that he didn't think a science writer had any business writing about legends. He'd been arrogant and patronizing. And worse, he hadn't even understood why she was angry. She seethed.

But she didn't want to pull Daku into this fight. The problem was between her and Mark. She wanted to keep it that way.

So she smoothed her expression, took deep breaths, and prepared to do battle on another field, her newspaper.

She had just met with Daku's grandfather, interviewing him about the Crow legends. She didn't want anything more to do with Mark, but she needed his scientific knowledge to help explain the science that might have triggered the legends. There was usually truth behind the enduring stories. Like, had this star flared brightly at another time?

Most importantly, Daku had bonded with Mark big time. And with her. And the adults with this great kid. She was trapped for the duration. She just had to get through the next couple days without killing Mark. That would set a bad example for Daku.

* * *

She almost tripped over what looked like a pile of blankets next to Mark's telescope. "Whoa, there, milady," Mark said softly, laughter in his voice as usual. "Don't want to wake the kid."
Molly bit off her words mid-retort. Mark turned on the low beam of his flashlight, showing her Daku curled up in Mark's sleeping bag, sound asleep.

"He wanted to stay with us, wanted to stay awake all night, actually. You can see how well that worked out. But I gather his family is comfortable with him sleeping outside nearby. They are a people most easy with the land."

She heard laughter in Mark's voice again. Not laughter against Daku or his people. Just, a kind of bemused pleasure with the twists of this world. It was the same laughter that made her so mad when directed at her. Not laughter against her either, she realized.

She sighed. This was an impossible situation. How could she want to punch and cuddle the same man at the same time?

"What's wrong?"

"Why would you think anything was wrong?" she snapped, irritated again.

"Oh, I don't know. The clenched fists. The fire in the eyes. The clipped tones."

She snorted. Lovely. He was making her laugh again. She reminded herself why she was upset.

"Okay. I think you are one of the most arrogant, bossy men on this planet, and that says a lot."

"Wait a minute! What brought all this on?" There was no hidden laughter this time. He actually sounded a little hurt. And a little angry. This was more like it. She felt like a good fight.

"You want things to go your way. You're all gallant, but you don't ask first. You decide for me."

"Is this still about me taking your bags?" he asked incredulously.

"Of course not. Or not entirely. It's just an example. It's your whole attitude. You chose where we would eat and set the timetable. Which does make some sense, I realize. You've been here longer and know the lay of the land. But still. You don't ask.

"But what makes me the maddest is how patronizing you can be. You probably don't even realize it."

He frowned. "I don't realize it. Do you think maybe you could be just a tad too sensitive? Just a tad, of course. And maybe, just maybe, looking for a fight?"

She clenched her fists. "So this is all me? There's no arrogance in you?"

"Well, I sure haven't been patronizing to you. What's that all about?"

She almost spat. "Well how about, 'This article is not worthy of you. It's not science'!"

"Ah. Okay, it isn't. If you want to write a fluff piece, that's one thing. It was very nice fluff. But it shouldn't be part of your science column. Myths have no business in science. People will think you're embracing all the legends."

"Oh, don't be an ass. Readers aren't dumb. They know I'm not saying this is scientific fact. That doesn't mean it's not worthy of attention."

"Okay. I agree that it's interesting. But it's not science. It doesn't belong in a science column. That's all I'm saying."

"Of course it does. The human factor definitely belongs in science. And furthermore, how do you explain all this? You have to admit, this star is the center of quite a lot of stories, world-rocking, magical stories."

"It is, I admit that. Okay, it's interesting. But you shouldn't have just left it with the myths. You should be explaining the science facts too."

"Well, if you'd get off your high horse, you'd discover that I plan to. I'm writing several stories a day. I was planning to interview you to see if you could explain how legends about this star have been around for so long. And if it could be the Christmas star. The stories all go together. But now. Now I don't want to talk to you anymore."

"Well, maybe I don't want to talk to you either."

They glared at each other.

"So. You want to look through my telescope?"

"Yes."

They kept glaring. His mouth twitched. She giggled. Oh crud, she couldn't believe she'd actually giggled. She sounded like a sick goose.

"If you aren't the most impossible woman!"

"Right back at 'ya. Only, man -- impossible man!"

"When this supernova/magic star story is over, do you think you could take some vacation time? We could explore Australia together. Or Denver. Or Iowa. Wherever you'd want to go. I'd like to spend some time with you. Get to know you better."

Molly stepped back, startled, suddenly overcome with shyness. Where had this come from? Was he for real? "Are you serious? We don't even know each other."

His background laughter was there again, peeking out around the corners of his voice. "Well, that's kind of the whole point. I want to. Know you better, I mean."

"Why? I mean, I haven't exactly been a dream companion lately, especially not with you."

"Oh, you are beyond my dreams. Much, much finer than my wildest dreams."

She stared at him, dumbfounded.

He reached out, gently brushed a long curl back behind her ear. He cupped her face, stroking her cheek gently with his thumb. All laughter gone from his face. Just a kind of hopeful wonder. *He* was looking at *her* this way. She was disconcerted. And ready to run. She started to stammer out an excuse.

He leaned forward and kissed her, tentatively, making sure she was okay with it. She dissolved into spangles of elemental matter, floating among the stars. His arms tightened around her, passion knocking out everything but blissful sensation.

He pulled away, looking down at her, still holding her. She moaned in protest. She moved into his wonderful hard chest again. She didn't want space between them. She stood on tiptoes, her fingers stroking the planes of his face, her kissing him this time. His arm around her waist. She never wanted this to stop.

Again, it was Mark who pulled away, still holding tight. "Hey, love. Beautiful, beautiful Molly."

He stroked her hair, gently. Oh lovely! Nobody ever played with her hair. He kissed her gently, all over her face and neck and arms and hands. And stopped again.

What torture was this? Why did he keep stopping?

"Why do you keep stopping?"

Laughter in his voice again. And regret. And hope. And tightly controlled passion. "Because we're in the middle of a crowd of star-gazers, and there is a little boy sleeping practically under our feet, and, unfortunately, we both have jobs to do this starry, starry night.

"Now. About that vacation…"

She laughed, but backed off a little. "I don't know. This is awfully fast."

He tightened his arms around her, then stepped back, holding her lightly at arm's length. "It doesn't seem that fast to me.

Seems like I've been waiting for you my whole life. There's no pressure though."

A choked little laugh. She stepped back a bit farther, but still touching him. She couldn't bear not to touch him now. Couldn't bear to think of him leaving right now either. But she was beginning to feel a little panicked.

"Just think about it, okay. You don't have to decide now. This tr p would just be a baby step in our relationship."

"A baby step is exchanging e-mail addresses. Not taking off for parts unknown together."

He grinned at her, stroking her hair again. They were chest to ches again. How had that happened? He hadn't moved. Oh wait. She'd moved closer. Oh she was in so much trouble.

This time the kiss went on for a very long time.

Chapter 7

Molly was blown away. She had never seen anything like these stars. The night sky was blazing with otherworldly fire. The Milky Way stretched out in an endless glowing path through the skies. And there was the Crow family shining with luminous intensity, with Mrs. Crow, (Ms. Crow?), the new shining star, as radiant as the moon.

Molly herself was radiant with happiness, leaning against Mark as he did his astronomer thing. Later, he was going to teach her how to work the specially-designed camera/telescope device. For right now, she was too full of sensations. Didn't think she could concentrate on anything technical. Besides, he was in work mode. She was supposed to be in work mode.

She kept panicking about going away together, but then they'd touch, and everything would fall gently into place. Just brushing against his arm was enough to right the world.

She was so confused. And scared. Trying to stay practical in the face of the hope pushing its way into her life.

"Young lady."

Molly'd heard that voice before. But it barely registered, and she forgot about it almost as soon as she'd heard it.

Snap. She felt a sharp sting across her hand.

What the...? She swam out of her mindfield, back into the desert night. Oh no. It was the mission lady who'd sat next to Mark on the plane. She'd been harassing the star tourists with her message this whole day. Now she was onto them. She was holding a pamphlet mid-strike, honing onto Molly's hand again. Molly jumped aside.

"You're that reporter who wrote about those heresies, aren't you?"

Molly stared at her, dumbfounded. "Um, what?"

"About the crow god and goddess."

Ah. "Not exactly gods, really."

"Heresy! Don't deny it. You wrote those stories."

"Not denying the writing part. You just got your facts wrong. Is there a problem?"

The woman sputtered. "The problem is, you shouldn't have written about these, these lies!"

"Wow. Everybody seems to have a problem with these stories."

Mark chomped down on a laugh. He'd come up next to her during the harangue. "Different problems," he said dryly.

"Ha!" She elbowed him. "A skunk by any other name…"

"Would smell like a rose?" he asked hopefully.

She narrowed her eyes at him, biting her lips to stop the smile.

"Young lady!"

"Ma'am?"

"I demand you print a retraction immediately. Tell the world this star is not some crow! This star is heralding the new Christmas story. A new start for mankind. Bringing in a story about some mystical crow lady just makes it even harder to convince people of the truth. It's ridiculous, primitive superstition."

"You are ridiculous!"

Oh no. Daku had heard this. He was awake and furious, standing and confronting the woman.

Molly and Mark exchanged dismayed glances.

"And we aren't primitive either. The story is true. Crow is real."

Molly put her arm around Daku.

The woman looked even more upset. Molly got ready to defend Daku against this bitter, crazy woman.

"I'm sorry, young man. I didn't mean your people were primitive. I was just referring to the story. And it's only primitive because this star's appearance now is what matters."

Molly and Mark exchanged glances again, this time of surprise. They'd been quick to judge the crazy lady too. Well, she was crazy. But not mean. Maybe.

Molly felt Daku relax against her. His usual exuberance bounced back. "That's okay. We're used to crazy Westerners."

"Hey!" Mark and Molly chimed in together.

Daku shot them a triumphant grin, and then stiffened suddenly, letting out a little gasp.

"Mulga!" he said sharply.

"What?" The three adults looked at him in concerned confusion.

"A liru." Daku was obviously frightened, unable to remember the English words.

Mark took a step towards Daku, stopped abruptly when Daku yelled. "No! Stop! Don't move! It's liru. I can't think of the English. On the ground by that rock!"

They all froze.

"I don't see…" Molly began.

"Snake!" The woman screamed.

This time they all registered the huge sinuous form uncoiling before them, right in front of Daku.

"Snakes don't come out at night," Mark said.

"And yet, here it is," Molly said quietly.

"This one does, if it's hot out," Daku whispered.

"Is it dangerous?" Mark whispered back.

"Oh, yes. People die from the mulga bite all the time."

The four people stood immobilized.

The snake raised its head.

"Should we back up?" Mark asked. "Will movement make it attack?"

"We should move very slowly away from it. It only attacks when it feels threatened. Otherwise mulga just want to live their own lives. We're safe if we don't do anything to make it nervous," Daku said.

"We come in peace," Mark said.

"Nice snake. Pretty snake." Molly whispered.

Daku backed up. One step. Two. Then his foot slipped on the sleeping bag. His legs flew out from under him, straight at the snake. The snake curved its head like a cobra, hissing, rising to strike.

Daku yelled.

Fast as thought, the snake lunged at him.

"No!" Molly screamed, jumping in front of Daku, Mark jumping in front of them both. The missionary lady, screaming bloody murder, jumped in front of Daku from the other side. Daku toppled backwards. The adults slammed into each other, going down in a wild scrambling ball of limbs, all of them hollering and screaming at once. The snake lunged forward again.

And was snatched mid-strike by a giant crow. It flew away, cawing raucously, the furious snake writhing in its claws. They could hear the triumphant caws echoing through the skies long after it vanished from sight.

Stunned, they stared at each other, frozen again. They all started to scramble upright, but fell back again, sliding on the slippery sleeping bag into a tighter ball, their tangled limbs getting in everyone else's way. And then, the stern, fierce missionary lady giggled. Mark, Molly and Daku dissolved into laughter, and the missionary's giggles exploded into loud whoops. Mark reached out a free arm, pulling Daku into the happy ball.

Molly snuggled closer to Mark, watching the glorious reds wash across the dawn sky. Daku was asleep beside them again, away from the snake's resting place this time. The missionary had gone back to her group, her worldview shimmering with change, her belief in the importance of the star reinforced, even so. Daku had been triumphant too. It was Crow who'd saved them, after all.

As for herself, she'd been confused about her feelings before. She wasn't anymore. When Mark had jumped in front of her and Daku, she'd been filled with terror. For Mark. The dope. Why did he have to be so heroic anyway? Jumping in front of her like that. It was one thing to protect a child. But he shouldn't have been risking his life for hers. She would have yanked him to safety if she'd had the time, or strength. She would rather be bitten herself. To think that one bite could have put an end to this funny, gentle, infuriating, frustrating, complex, gorgeous, brilliant man. What if she'd lost him?

As soon as she thought her editor would be in, she was calling the paper, asking for a long vacation. She was going on the journey with Mark. She wasn't letting this chance pass her by. Really, what if she'd lost him? She shivered.

Mark tightened his arms, pulling her closer.

"I think you were right," Mark said.

"Oh good. Right about what?"

"You should be writing about the different ways people are looking at this star. There do seem to be miracles afoot. I mean, that crow does not seem like any bird I've ever seen. It saved our lives, or at least one of our lives. And it brought us together."

Molly blushed, glad it was still dark. "Maybe we're all right."

"Right about what?"

"Maybe the star is Lady Crow, and a herald of a savior, and an exploding star, all in one. No reason it can't be all this and more, all at once. Today is Christmas, after all. Miracles are traditional."

"So they are. And speaking of miracles. Molly, I don't want you to vacation with me."

She started to draw back, surprised at how deeply hurt she was. His arms tightened, holding her gently but firmly.

"Wait. I don't want just a vacation with you. I want a honeymoon. Molly, will you marry me? The real miracle is that I've fallen in love. Overnight. Against all odds. I love you, lovely Molly. Marry me. Please. Please. Please."

She started to laugh, to draw back, to move forward, all at once. Her cautionary armor sprang back into place, and then, poofed into dust.

She sprang forward, holding his dear face, kissing him deeply.

He held her apart. "Is that yes? Are you kissing me yes?"

"Oh, yes. Yes. And yes."

The dawn blasted out all around them, but it was wasted on them. They only had eyes for each other.

A big black crow let out a caw the two lovers didn't even hear. He folded his wings, tucked his head into his chest, and settled in beside the boy dreaming of visiting America and running barefoot through the warm snow. Well, why not? It was miracle time.

Blame it on the Christmas Lights

By

Karyn Cole

"I hate to tell you this, Lucy," Dr. Heath took off her glasses and set them on her desk. "But it looks like your ovaries aren't working."

"Not working? But I'm getting my period. TWICE every month. That's why I came in for a checkup. I want them to work *less*. In fact, I'd like them to take a friggin' vacation!"

"Yes, well, there's probably an explanation. My guess is that because you aren't ovulating- an egg isn't being released- the uterine wall doesn't know when to shed. So it just gets thicker until finally it starts shedding randomly and…"

Lucy held up her hand. "So what does that mean? I don't ovulate, I can't have kids?"

"It will be difficult for you to get pregnant. You won't know from time to time whether an egg has actually been released. I'm not saying it can't happen, I'm just saying you're going to have to plan for it. And I can walk you through that when you're ready. It's something to think about at your age, Lucy. Do you think you want kids?"

Lucy stared at her doctor, open-mouthed. She was only 30. She hadn't even thought about having kids, yet. . "I…I mean, yes. I want kids, I just…oh my god."

Dr. Heath patted Lucy's hand. "Don't worry too much. There's a lot we can do these days to help the process along."

When Dr. Heath left, Lucy didn't know whether to cry or throw something. She opted to get dressed. There wasn't really anything she could change, and besides, she had places to be.

It was December 15th. The Christmas marathon had begun and she'd barely left the starting line. She had to focus on the holiday ahead. She hadn't even begun to shop, and with ten days left, her options would be limited. She needed to focus on her "to do" list.

First, she had to pick up her baby brother at the airport, followed by a quick parental meet-up to get rid of her brother as quickly as possible. Lucy loved him, but didn't have time for tales of his college conquests and requests for money. At some point she had to find time to make a gift for her baby nephew, who would hate it, but cry cutely when forced to wear it. Then, she had to find gifts for her best friends and work partners. They were a mixed gaggle who had known each other since college and thrown in together to start their own business. Even though they saw each other every day, they got together often for girls' nights out and to shop. The group was a bit nutty, a lot naughty and the only fun she had on a regular basis. They'd all agreed to a thirty dollar limit, but rarely did they stick to their agreement. Lucy hated having to guess what they wanted. She was terrible at picking out gifts.

"Shit," she mumbled as she got into her car and headed toward the mall. A part of her wanted a time-out to cry about her broken lady parts, but there just wasn't enough time. It was almost Christmas, for Christ's sake. She needed to be jolly.

* * *

Lucy made it to her apartment, arms loaded down with shopping bags and a twelve-pack of diet soda. The entire complex was lit up with the Christmas lights decorating people's balconies. All except one. Her balcony was dark, and it was going to stay that way.

"Bah humbug," she murmured. She wasn't about to drink the Christmas Kool-aid and spend money on unnecessary lights for a balcony she never used.

By the time she'd stumbled her way up the stairs to her third floor apartment, her phone was vibrating in her purse. She managed to maneuver inside with all of her items and reached for the phone as she unceremoniously dropped her bags by the front door.

"Yes, Ma, what do you need?" She put the phone on speaker and started shedding layers while her mother talked.

"I don't know what to get your brother and sister-in-law. I'm starting to panic. Do you have any ideas?

"Nope. I don't know what to get them either," she answered as she poked her head into her favorite sweatshirt.

"They just have everything. More than your father and I ever had, that's for sure," her mother went on.

Lucy blew out a breath that sent her bangs into the air. It was time to do what she did best: rationalize. "Mom, their baby has a mullet. So they clearly don't have everything, like common sense, for instance."

Laughter echoed through the phone and Lucy gave herself a mental high-five. Before her mother could start in on anything else, she decided she'd better sign off. "I gotta go, Ma. I have a ton of shit to do."

"You'll never get a man with that potty mouth of yours, Lucille Marie."

Lucy rolled her eyes. She could almost see her mother's narrowed, judgy eyes. She ought to tell her mom that men liked hearing dirty things come out of her mouth, but she didn't want to start another bout of drama, so she let it go. "I know. You're right. I love you. Goodnight."

The call was done. Her sweatpants were on and now she could collapse onto her couch. As soon as she was nested in the cushions and blankets, she took a deep, soothing breath. The apartment was dark and silent. She should have been relieved. Instead, Lucy was just a little bit lonely.

* * *

"What's with the grump face? You look like you haven't slept in a year."

"Thanks for that lovely compliment, Claudia. You're looking fabulous today as well," Lucy offered with a glare. It was true, Claudia looked good. Her long dark hair was pulled into a sleek ponytail and she was wearing a cute dress with matching tights and kick-ass boots, something Lucy only wished she could pull off. If they weren't such good friends, Lucy would despise her.

"Sorry," Claudia shrugged. "I just meant you look a little rough. No harm. I swear I come in peace. With diet soda." Claudia held out a cold can of Lucy's favorite beverage, and in Lucy's eyes the world seemed brighter. She took the can and opened the tab. Once she'd taken a big gulp, she sighed and turned to her friend and co-worker.

"Sorry for snapping at you. You're seriously a life-saver." She took another drink. She couldn't stay mad when plied with diet soda. And she *did* look horrible. She'd seen it in the mirror that morning. Her blonde hair was in a messy bun and she'd had to put her glasses on instead of her usual contacts. Plus, she'd over-indulged in ice cream the night before and resorted to her frumpy khakis and a blah blue polo shirt for work.

Claudia took a seat on the edge of Lucy's desk. "You're welcome. Now, spill. What's with the dark circles?"

"Damn. I was really hoping people would mistake those for smoky eyes," she joked. "But seriously, Claud, you'd look like this too if your entire apartment building was suddenly Santa's Bordello."

"Come again?"

"Oh, they did. Again and again. It happened all night. I tried to sleep in my bedroom but the Hallelujah chorus from next door kept sounding. So then I moved to the living room and heard more 'Oh gods' and 'Jesus, please,' than in a Baptist church."

Claudia looked incredulous.

"I'm not exaggerating. It's those damn Christmas lights they put up. Now everyone is in the holiday spirit and I'm surrounded by a bunch of 'ho ho ho's.'"

"And you've become the Grinch." Claudia smirked, seeming to enjoy Lucy's pain.

"I'm not a Grinch. I just don't think there is a point to this good cheer."

"Holidays give people an excuse to be happy. Who wouldn't be excited about presents and time off work? I know that would put *me* in the mood for some nookie."

"Ugh. Whatever. I don't need those things to be happy and full of cheer."

"True. I generally replace holiday cheer with beer. Now that's amazing."

Lucy grinned. "See, you do get it!"

"Yes!" Claudia nodded. "I should get back to my desk. But before I go, Grinchy-poo, if you change your mind about being cheerful, you can always come to that party my neighbor is having. There will be beer."

"Is this the cute neighbor who's in anesthesia school or the guy who throws his dead fish in your yard?"

Lucy was rewarded with a 'duh' look for the question. "They're roommates. So they're throwing the party together. I'm sure that each of them has lots of single male friends. If not, you can have fish boy and I'll take the guy with access to the good drugs."

Lucy laughed. "You're such a good friend to me. Sounds like a solid plan. I could use some 'get-my-drink-on' time."

"Excellent. It's decided then. You, me and a houseful of men, whose quality has yet to be determined."

"High-five!" They slapped hands somewhat limply and got back to work.

* * *

An hour before the party, Lucy was still in her work clothes. She wanted to call Claudia and cancel so she could drown herself in the sweatpants calling to her from her bedroom floor. She had a million other things she could be doing and this party should have been last on the list.

Her phone chirped to let her know she had a text.

Claudia: You are not getting out of this. I've been plucked and waxed to an inch of my life. I'm not going alone. Shave your legs to your knees and get your ass over here.

With Claudia's text in her head, Lucy said a silent farewell to her sweatpants and went to get ready.

* * *

Three glasses of champagne weren't doing anything to make Lucy have fun. In fact, she was yawning, when she wasn't glaring at the too-bright Christmas lights. The party was crowded, full of couples being all lovey-dovey under the mistletoe. It turned out that the anesthesia guy had a girlfriend and they had a bunch of couple-friends instead of just guy-friends. Nice people. But all of the love was going to make her throw up.

"I don't even see the fish-thrower," Claudia frowned and drank the rest of her champagne. "I feel like I'm wasting a perfectly good outfit and hair day."

"Sad." Lucy shook her head in mock disappointment. She did understand about the outfit thing, though. She'd spent a half-hour deciding on her skinny jeans and sparkly sweater. She'd even taken her hair out of its usual bun. It was a wasted effort, so far.

Claudia glared at her over the top of her glass. "It *is* sad, you sarcastic Sally. Fish boy is kind of cute."

"Well, that remains to be seen. Ten minutes ago you thought Karaoke Ken over there was hot." She referred to the gentleman over by the snack table shoveling cheese puffs into his mouth like they were going out of style.

"He was singing Neil Diamond. You know that's my weakness." Claudia's eyes sparkled and grew wide, a possessive hand on her chest.

"Sure, sure. Listen…ten more minutes of this and I've got to go. I'm working tomorrow in the a.m. and then I have to finish wrapping presents in the afternoon." She wasn't really working; she just couldn't stand another minute of watching everyone else be so damn googily-eyed.

"Fine. Be responsible. I guess I'll go too. No sense trying to hang around a love fest when there isn't even anyone to like." Claudia looked disappointed and for a second Lucy felt guilty. But then she caught sight of a couple linking their arms to drink their champagne, and she knew she was seconds away from the pain in her head becoming an unsightly eye twitch.

"Christmas lights do strange thing to people," Lucy said in her best 'I-told-you-so' voice.

Claudia rolled her eyes. "Whatever, Grinch. I'll go grab our coats."

Lucy almost sagged with relief that Claudia agreed without much fuss. She could practically feel the warmth of her sweatpants. With a grin of triumph on her face she turned to set down her glass and nearly collided with a hard chest.

"Whoa. Watch where you're going," a deep voice chided.

She pursed her lips, ready to tell him to shove it, but decided at the last second to let it go. It was Christmas after all. She could play nice. Besides, she was leaving to go home to her empty apartment where she could be alone...

"Oops. Sorry," she smiled and tilted her head up.

The fake smile broadened and became sincere. "Oh my god! Jake Leighton?"

A tall, dark haired, full-fledged man stood in front of her, grinning back. "Hello to you, too, Lucy Potter."

Just like that, Lucy was in high school again, pining over a soft-spoken brooder who had no trouble getting girls. His brown hair was shorter than she remembered, his jaw line sharper, and he was better looking, which was saying a lot.

"How are you? What are you up to? What are you doing here?" Lucy's questions shot out like bullets and Jake's eyebrows rose at the impact. He kept smiling.

"Good, trouble, and trying to find trouble."

Lucy laughed, the sound joined by the baritone of his amusement. She shrugged. "Sorry…I'm just, so surprised to see you. What's it been…like ten years?"

"I'd say yes, but you don't look much older than the last time I saw you, Lucy."

"Seeing as age is now a sensitive issue, I'm going to take that as a compliment. But if you mean I look dorky, I might have to throw my drink in your face," she teased.

He laughed and held up his hands. "No. Definitely not dorky. Quite the opposite. You look great. You always were cute."

Lucy kept smiling but cringed inwardly at the 'cute' part. Puppies were cute. Two-year-olds were cute (until they threw a tantrum). Calling her cute put her right back into a category she'd been trying to escape since high school: the "friend".

"So what do you do now?" he asked and took a drink from the beer bottle in his hand.

"Exotic dancer," she deadpanned.

It was a good thing she was short or he would have spit beer in her face.

"Shit, Lucy. I'm sorry…I…" He shook his head and a dark brown lock of hair flopped onto his forehead. He awkwardly patted her hair with a napkin.

"No," she waved the apology off and his napkin. "It's my fault. I should really know better. Not everyone gets my sense of humor."

He chuckled and looked down at his shirt, patting at the wet spots. "I should have remembered how funny you always were."

Her face grew warm. It was another semi-compliment. Nice to be remembered for being funny, but it wasn't like she'd been the class clown. Couldn't he have remembered something else? Like her smile? Her dentist said her teeth were amazing. And they were all hers. Probably her best feature, but they always went unnoticed. Sigh. "Yeah, well. That's me, funny Lucy." She downed the rest of her champagne in a large swallow.

He was still smiling. A dimple appeared in his left cheek and she wanted to stick her tongue in it. She was a sucker for dimples.

"Funny Lucy," he repeated, the tone low and almost affectionate and enough to produce a spine-tingling shiver. Lucy felt her cheeks get even warmer. She was going to start sweating soon, she just knew it. Where the hell was Claudia with their coats?

"I'm uh…not really an exotic dancer," she offered lamely.

"You sure? I mean, I thought I recognized you from my friend's bachelor party." He squinted and pretended to look her up and down. Her cheeks were flaming, she was sure.

"Ha. Ha. Okay. Sure. I guess the truth is that I'm a retired exotic dancer. I gave it up. I'm an event planner now."

"What does an event planner do?"

Lucy smirked. "Oh, you know... plan events."

He laughed first then took a pull from his beer. "Ok. Ok. Stupid question. I meant, what kind of events?"

"You name it, we plan it: weddings, birthdays, anniversaries, baptisms, divorces, and dog adoptions. There have even been a few 'yay, you made parole' parties. We're not too picky. My friend Gretchen calls us the whores of party planning. If there's money involved, we'll do it."

More laughter. Lucy supposed if nothing else went right with her life, she would at least be funny.

"So should I be telling you 'good job' for this event?" He was looking over her head and she turned, following the direction of his gaze to where Karaoke Ken was now digging barbequed weenies out of a crock-pot, spilling sauce all over.

Lucy couldn't help it. She snorted. "It's definitely reminding me of one of the parole parties. But no, this isn't one of ours. To be honest, I don't even know these people. My friend Claudia lives next door. She's around here somewhere." She let her eyes wander the room to look for Claudia and spotted her over by the back wall. She wasn't holding any coats. She was too busy making out with someone Lucy couldn't see. "Are you here with anyone?"

Jake shook his head. "Nah…I'm flying solo."

The way he said it made Lucy laugh. She couldn't help it. "You sound like a sad bird. Solo isn't so bad. I was just making sure I wasn't going to get my eyes clawed out by a jealous girlfriend. This party isn't exactly single-girl friendly."

"I noticed something like that earlier. Everyone is attached to someone." His eyes stayed intently on her and the dimple reappeared.

"It's weird, right? It's like they're only allowed to mingle in pairs. And if you try breaking into a group, you're some kind of home wrecking devil." She knew she was talking too much but Jake was so attractive and he was listening to everything she said and she just couldn't make the words stop. "There's this girl over by the punch who's been giving me the evil eye all night. Like she thinks I'm over here plotting to take her nasty-ass boyfriend away. Uh…I'm sorry, but I don't' want meat from somebody else's plate, thank you very much."

Lucy covered her mouth with her hand. What was she thinking? "Sorry. Too much booze and I get lippy," she tried to explain. His face wasn't giving anything away. She couldn't tell what he was thinking and it only made her talk more to fill the awkward silence before it began. "No…I should be honest. I'm not nice and I'm always lippy. I just get more so when I drink."

Jake's whole face split into a grin. "You are....*exactly* like I would have expected if I knew what to expect, Lucy Potter. You want to get out of here?"

Her mouth dropped open a little. He wanted to leave with her?

She thought about her sweatpants, but instead of comfort, her belly tightened, butterflies dancing around inside as Jake smiled at her again. Ten years was a long time. They could certainly catch up. There would be no harm in that.

"We can go grab a coffee," he suggested when she didn't answer right away.

"Uhm…yeah. Coffee sounds good." She hated coffee. It made her gag. But she'd fake it or something. He wanted to talk more and maybe the night would end just a little less lonely.

* * *

They were at the local pancake house, closing the place down over plates of scrambled eggs and chocolate chip pancakes.

"God, this makes me so happy," Lucy said around a forkful of whipped cream-topped chocolate chip pancake goodness.

"You're so easy," Jake joked.

"You have no idea." It came out more suggestive then she'd intended, but instead of correcting the impression, she forked another bite and savored it.

"Tell me more about party planning. I bet you have some stories."

Lucy waited until she'd finished her bite. "I do."

Jake looked at her expectantly and Lucy blushed as she closed her mouth around another bite of pancake. She chewed quickly. "You want me to tell you one. Gotcha."

He watched her, elbows on the table, hands folded together in front of him.

"So, this one time, a new DJ showed up to replace the regular DJ. The newbie decided to play Celine Dion and the crowd rioted. When he tried to change the song, he was nervous and broke the equipment. The song kept playing in loop. He ended up hiding under the table to keep from being killed."

"What'd you do?"

Lucy shrugged. "I unplugged the sound system. Set up an ipod."

Jake's shoulders fell. "That's it? No fighting? No threats?"

"Sorry. I never said my stories were *good.*"

His husky laugh made that dimple appear again and the combination made her feel like her stomach was going to burst from butterflies.

Lucy went on with their discussion. "Tell me more about you. Last I heard, you were trying to free people in Tibet or something."

"Nah. I was going through a phase. I snapped out of it when I realized how bad I smelled."

"Mhmm. I trust you've showered this evening."

"Definitely."

"Ok, so you're back in town and taking over your dad's business. How did you get roped into that?"

"Guilt."

"Guilt?"

He nodded. "The old-fashioned, familial kind."

She held up a hand. "Say no more. I know exactly what you mean." Without pausing, she barreled on. "But I have to say I'm glad the guilt worked. It's really great seeing you again."

"You too."

There had been lots of small pauses in their conversation as each of them tried to find points of conversation. But now they both just smiled, enjoying each other. It had been a long time since Lucy had been out with someone attractive like Jake and genuinely enjoyed herself. But he was easy to talk to and laugh with and he didn't seem to mind that she was a little bit goofy.

Jake looked down at his watch. "It's getting late...you want to get out of here?" He looked up at her expectantly.

"Can you take me to get my car?" She hoped he would say something about seeing each other again. Unless she'd read him wrong and he wasn't interested. He'd been so nice and she was pretty sure he was flirting.

"Absolutely. Let's go." He pulled himself from the booth and put on his coat. Then he helped her up and held her coat for her. She wanted to pinch herself. How many guys were that good-looking and actual gentlemen, too?

For a brief second she thought about what might be wrong with Jake. How could he be so smart and handsome and nice and still single? The thoughts disappeared as she felt the slide of his fingers through hers and their palms pressed together. Right now she didn't care, she just wanted to see what might happen next.

* * *

When the alarm went off the next morning, Lucy's first thought was a groan. Mornings were not her friend. As her brain started working, she realized she didn't have to be anywhere until afternoon. She closed her eyes, ready to slip back into her dreams when the bed dipped and the covers shifted.

Her eyes snapped open. Christmas lights blinked outside the window. This wasn't her place.

"Hey...I gotta get going. I've got to meet my dad down at the store in like twenty minutes." Jake's husky voice met her ears and...

Lucy froze.

The night before came back to her and her face flamed with the memory. It hadn't been a dream. She turned over, clutching the blankets to her chest. "Uhm...ok. Uh...see you?"

Lucy didn't know how to do this. She didn't usually bring guys home with her, let alone to Claudia's house, which was where they'd ended up.

Jake was sitting up in the bed, looking down at her, waiting for something.

"So...I'll just...uh... You, can just, uhm, wait here for me?"
She sat up and hoped he'd turn away while she maneuvered her
naked self out of bed. Keeping the blanket clutched to her chest,
she grabbed up the clothes that were strewn around the room. She
could feel Jake's eyes on her and wanted to fill the awkward
silence with words, but she had none. Instead she slipped passed
him into the bathroom.

Her party clothes were rumpled and gross but she put them
back on anyway, the whole time wondering just how she'd let this
happened. One minute they'd been laughing and singing along to
a song in his car and then he'd pulled into Claudia's driveway and
she was going to tell him to call her, but before the words could
leave her mouth he'd kissed her and well, clearly it hadn't ended
with the kissing. She'd been planning to spend the night at
Claudia's, she just hadn't planned on having a guest.

With a deep breath, Lucy left the bathroom and found Jake
sitting on the edge of the bed, waiting for her.

"So this is awkward, right?" she blurted.

Jake's mouth quirked into a smile, complete with dimple.

Lucy blinked. "Hide your dimple," she told him. "I can't
handle your dimple this morning."

Jake laughed. "Is that your secret turn on? Dimples?
Cause last night you wouldn't shut up about Christmas lights."

Lucy rubbed her eyes as her feet carried her to the bed and
she sat next to him. "In my defense, Claudia has the Christmas
lights market cornered."

"I feel a little weird that we ended up here," Jake admitted. "Are you sure Claudia won't mind?"

"Yeah, no. She knew I was going to stay over last night if we drank too much. If anyone should be worried, it should be me. I'm going to get so much shit about our hookup. Because I never do this. Never." Lucy's head found her way to Jake's shoulder for a second.

"You might have mentioned that a few times as well." His shoulder bumped hers and when she turned her head, he was grinning at her, dimple working full force. She couldn't help it. She leaned up and he leaned down and they were kissing.

"I think we should keep seeing each other," he admitted between kisses.

Lucy nodded, her nose brushing against his, their lips barely grazing as she spoke a breathless "Me, too."

Ten minutes later, they were still kissing goodbye and then Jake had to go or he was going to be late. When Lucy found Claudia in the kitchen, her friend was enjoying a cup of coffee and bowl of cereal.

"So *you* had a good time last night." Claudia stated around a mouthful of whole grain.

"Yes." Lucy sat down at the table. "Do you have any diet coke?"

Claudia nodded and jerked her head toward the fridge. "You can only have it if you spill details."

Lucy's nose crinkled. "Eew. I don't think so."

"I don't mean those details." Claudia rolled her eyes. "I heard enough last night to make a good guess about that part of things. I mean, who is he and how did you get from wanting to leave the party to hooking up with tall, dark and sexy in my spare bedroom."

"I used to have a big crush on him in high school. He's back to help run his dad's pharmacy. We're going to see what happens."

"Good for you." Claudia went back to her cereal and Lucy stood up to go the fridge. When she came back, Claudia was pulling her hair back into a ponytail and Lucy noticed a bruise on her friend's neck.

"So...it looks like I wasn't the only one who got some action last night. I think you need to spill." Lucy popped the top on her diet soda and propped her chin on her wrist, grinning as she waited for Claudia to fess up.

"I may have had my own visitor last night."

"Really? Looks like your Christmas lights worked."

"Hey. I had those up before you decided they were some kind of strange Christmas aphrodisiac. If they happened to work, so be it." She was looking at the wall like it was the most interesting thing she'd ever seen.

"Do I get to hear any more? Or is it private?"

Claudia's shoulders sagged. "It...it was Peter."

She didn't have to say any more. Lucy knew all about Peter. Claudia's ex-boyfriend always seemed to show up unexpectedly. He never stayed long, but it was always enough to make Claudia think they'd have a chance. Then he'd leave without a word and Claudia would have to nurse her broken heart.

"I made him leave. I...I woke up this morning and just couldn't handle repeating the pattern. I don't want him at all if it's not going to be forever. I deserve better than that." A tear escaped down Claudia's cheek, and Lucy stood up and gave her friend a hug.

"You do deserve better. But I'm sorry."

Claudia sniffled and let out a watery laugh. "It's fine. I can handle it. Let's talk about something else."

"Well, I think Jake wants to hire us," Lucy offered.

"He doesn't think we're strippers, does he?"

"Funny. No. He wants to throw a retirement-slash-New Year's party for his dad. I told him we could work something out."

"Actually, that's perfect. Let me take care of it. I could use the busy work and then that will free you up to get your flirt on."

* * *

On Christmas Eve, Lucy kept checking her phone. Jake was texting her. They'd been seeing each other as much as possible. Most of the time he stayed at her place, and this was the most time they'd spent apart except for work.

Part of Lucy wished they could spend Christmas together, but she wasn't quite ready to introduce him to her crazy family.

"Why are you grinning?" Her brother asked as he plopped down next to her on the couch. She hid her phone and smiled at him.

"No reason. Just happy to be around everyone." It was a lie, actually. Their family Christmas had been full of arguing between her brothers. Lucy'd only been home for the day and she was tired of it.

"Whatever. Who are you texting?"

"No one. Where's your kid? I want to play with my nephew." She changed the subject. Talking about Braden was a safe topic and one sure to get her brother off on a tangent.

A few hours later, Lucy had a full-on headache. The squabbles between her siblings had continued until her mother had left the house and her dad had holed up in the basement. She'd ended up playing mediator and suggesting a haircut for Braden before leaving for the night. She would have stayed, but the couch hadn't been an appealing choice for sleeping and she wanted to be at home.

As she settled into bed that night, she sent a text to Jake.

Lucy: Why aren't we together tonight?

It didn't take him long to respond.

Jake: I don't know. Where are you?

Lucy: My place.

Jake: I'll be there in ten.

And he was.

Later, as they were falling asleep, Lucy decided it was the best Christmas she'd had in a long time.

* * *

"How are the plans for the retirement party going?" Lucy was in a meeting on Dec 26th, going over the different parties they had planned for the next few weeks. Claudia sat next to her, looking over her notes. "Plans are good. We settled on January 3rd instead of New Year's Eve. So we've got an extra couple of days. Venue is set, we booked one of the banquet rooms at the Avenue Hotel. I placed an order with the florist for some table bouquets, and we've got a cake ordered and some other hors d'oeuvres picked out. Should be good to go."

Lucy smiled at Claudia. The party would be great, she had no doubt. Although she was sort of nervous about it. Jake wanted her to be there, but not as a party planner. She was going to meet his parents that night, and the idea made her want to bury her head in the snow. At least the party would be lovely.

When the meeting ended, Claudia followed Lucy to her desk. "You still all lovey-dovey with Jake?" she asked casually and took a seat on top of the desk.

"Let's not bring up the L-word quite yet."

"He hasn't said it?"

Lucy rolled her eyes. "Why would he? It's only been a couple of weeks."

"But aren't you guys, like, living together and having sex all the time?"

"Yes, but...that doesn't mean he has to say it."

"But you want to say it, right?"

"Claudia...." Lucy didn't know how to answer that. She wasn't sure what she felt. She wanted to be with Jake as much as possible, but Love? She didn't know what that word meant, and she wasn't about to start throwing it around. "We don't have sex all the time."

"Whatever. You're like bunny rabbits. I'm surprised you aren't knocked up yet."

The words were a reminder of her doctor's appointment. She'd been avoiding thoughts on Dr. Heath's diagnosis. But she would have to face the reality of it sooner than later. And she was going to have to explain that reality to Jake at some point if they were going to stay together. What if he wanted kids? How would she live with herself if she was denying him something like that?

Later that night, Jake called and wanted to come over, but Lucy lied and told him she wasn't feeling well. She crawled into bed, ready to cry herself to sleep, but the buzzer for her apartment went off. She hit the talk button to ask who it was.

"Me."

Surprised, she pushed in the enter button and went to wait at her door. As soon as the knock came, she flung the door open.

Jake stood there, a sheepish grin on his face. "I know you said you don't feel well, but I thought maybe there was something I could do to help."

Lucy almost started bawling then, and when he opened his arms, she walked right into them. How was she ever going to give this up? Even if it was for Jake's own good.

* * *

Over the next few days, Lucy tried to tell herself that getting distance from Jake was necessary for both of them. It would hurt them both less when it was time to break up. And they would have to. There was no way Jake could live without kids. He'd brought it up too many times since they met, talking about how he was at a point in his life where having a family seemed right.

Dear Lord, it made her heart ache to think about it. She could almost picture their kids, a dark-haired little girl with her daddy's blue eyes and her mommy's perfect teeth. And then a little boy, with blond hair and a mohawk - Jake's idea, obviously. They'd be adorable and loveable and...

...they would never really exist. There could still be a dark-haired little girl in Jake's future, but it wouldn't be theirs.

The very thought of breaking up with Jake, even if it would be doing him a favor, made Lucy sick. She could barely stomach any kind of food and had given up diet soda because it only made her feel worse. She'd been blissfully happy, trapped in a love bubble. But the bubble was going to burst.

Even Claudia was picking up on Lucy's depressed mood. "We need a girl's night," she said over lunch. "You need a night away from Jake and I need a friend. What do you say?"

"Deal." Lucy was relieved at the idea. It was a good excuse for distance from Jake, one that didn't make her feel guilty for lying or playing it cool.

She met up with Claudia at her house that night.

"You've still got your Christmas lights up." She stomped the snow off her boots and then leaned over to kick them off. Claudia took her coat for her and Lucy followed her into the house.

"Yeah. I'm too lazy to take them down. Just felt kind of blah, lately, you know."

"I know exactly what you mean," Lucy admitted.

"Really? I would have thought you'd be too blissed out on love to feel blah right now."

Lucy shrugged and bit down on her bottom lip. To be honest, she felt more than blah. She'd been on the verge of tears for days. She was ready to break.

"How about something to drink? Then we can put the movie in and pretend to watch it," Claudia suggested. Lucy agreed and waited on the couch for Claudia to return. She was expecting wine but was surprised when her friend brought them both a glass of water.

She raised an eyebrow, curious at the drink choice.

Claudia took a deep breath and blurted out, "I'm pregnant."
Lucy started to cry.

* * *

It should have been Lucy comforting Claudia. Instead, Claudia was listening as Lucy's entire gyno appointment was relayed.

"Wow...I don't know what to say, Luce. Why didn't you talk about this sooner?"

"I didn't want to believe it was true, and now I'm just...I'm so happy for you," she sobbed and blew her nose. "But I'm selfish and it makes me sad for myself. And I have to tell Jake and...."

Claudia nodded, sympathy written all over her face. "I see. That's what's been making you sick, isn't it."

Lucy blew her nose again. "I just...I don't want to get to that moment where he has to end it because I can't give him babies. It will...it will devastate me."

Every time she blew her nose, it sounded like a horn blasting, but she was a mess of tears and snot and she just didn't care. "I wasn't even looking for this relationship, ya know? It just kind of found me and I never expected to..." she shuddered and breathed in "...to care so much about him and the future we could have. It's just..." another shudder.

Lucy knew she needed to get herself under control. They'd been focusing on her, when it was Claudia who had the real news.

"I'm sorry," Lucy told her friend and offered up a watery smile. "Tell me about you. How are you feeling?"

Claudia gave Lucy's shoulder a quick squeeze and then let out a sigh. "Well, I'm ok. A little shocked, but ok. I...I...wasn't planning this, obviously. But I'm happy about it. And before you ask, the baby's father is Pete."

"I figured. Have you told him?"

Claudia's smile turned upside down and she shook her head. "I'm not going to. I have no idea how to reach him and I just don't have the energy to track him down. If he wanted to be in my life, he would. I'm not going to use this baby to make it happen. So, I'm gonna be a single mom and I'm okay with it, really."

Lucy sniffled. "You know I'll help you, right? No matter what, you can count on me. Okay?"

"Thanks, Luce. I appreciate it. Really. Now...will you do something for me?"

"Sure, anything."

"Go find Jake and tell him right now. Get it over with, like ripping off a band-aid. It might hurt, but at least it will be done and you'll be able to move forward instead of making yourself sick with it."

"But I..."

"Do it, Lucy."

* * *

She found Jake at the pharmacy. He was working on inventory and surprised to see her. He let her in and led her toward the back break room. "I thought it was girls' night."

"It was, but I needed...I needed to talk to you." Lucy bit down on her bottom lip, trying to keep her tears at bay. This was hard. She didn't want to do this.

"What's up? Is something wrong?" Jake sat down across from her at the table. His dark hair was disheveled like he'd been running his fingers through it. His jaw had a day's worth of beard growth, enough to make her mouth red if they kissed.

Finally she met his gaze. The corners of his mouth were turned down, concern written in his eyes and with the furrow of his brow. She took a deep breath.

"I'm not sure I'll be able to have kids and I thought you should know."

"What?" He looked confused.

"I...well, the doctor told me that my ovaries don't work and I don't ovulate, so getting pregnant will be hard and you need to know that. Because if you can't deal with it, then we should end this now before either of us gets in too deep."

"Lucy..."

She held up her hand. "I just, I have to tell you this because I know you do want kids and I wish I could give them to you, but I'm just afraid that it won't happen. I don't want you to resent me. It would hurt too much. And you mean so much to me. You're like my best friend now and I don't want to lose that."

She was crying in earnest and Jake wasn't even looking at her.

"That's what you want? You want us to be friends?"

"Yes, if that's all we can be, then yes. I don't want to lose you from my life and I..."

"I can't just be your friend, Lucy. I love you. It would be too hard to..." His voice trailed off.

Lucy felt her heart breaking. "Okay. I-I gotta go. Have a nice life, Jake. And I really mean that," she managed through her tears.

* * *

She spent New Year's Eve on her couch. Her mother had called to invite her to a party at her grandparents', but Lucy was not up for familial company. Claudia was out of town visiting her parents to tell them her baby news. Lucy had decided she'd rather be alone with a pint of ice cream than celebrate the coming year. It would be shit and she'd be alone.

At least she had her sweatpants.

The thought wasn't as comforting as it had once been.

She couldn't even have the night with Dick Clark because he was dead and Ryan Seacrest just didn't cut it. It would be like trying to replace Jake. It just wouldn't ever be the same.

So she was left with movies. Her whole shelf was full of love stories, but love wasn't exactly high on her list of favorite things. She was avoiding romance movies and anything vaguely romantic. She couldn't even listen to the radio or read a book because romance was everywhere, and the truth was, it was crap. It made her sad.

So *Kill Bill* seemed more appropriate. Nothing like a little ass-kicking and gore to ring in the next year.

At midnight, she got a bevy of phone calls to tell her "Happy New Year." Nothing from Jake. Not that she'd expected him to call. They'd broken up. He should be living it up at some New Year's party with slutty girls in too-tight dresses. He could take one of them home and get her pregnant and live happily ever after.

She cried and her ice cream melted. Eyes swollen, she threw out the pint and decided she'd go get some more. This time she'd get the cookie dough.

It was snowing a bit, so she threw on her ugly black snow boots and zipped them over her sweatpants. She probably looked ridiculous, but didn't care. She grabbed her grey wool coat and pulled a maroon stocking cap down over her hair.

Keys in her mittened hands, she opened the door and stood face to face with Jake.

The keys dropped to the floor and her mouth opened, no words escaping.

"Can I come in?" he asked.

Lucy didn't know what to say, so she just nodded and let him walk inside.

He took several long strides into the living room where the TV was playing the after-hours party from Times Square.

He turned to look at her, and she still didn't know what to say.

"Lucy..."

"I was going to get ice cream." She could have hit herself in the head for telling him that. It's not like he couldn't tell she was going out. "For my pity party," she added. Like that made it any better.

His face, which had been tight with determination, softened. The right side of his mouth lifted into a sad, half-grin. "Why were you having a pity party?"

Lucy shrugged, the stiff shoulders of her coat making the movement awkward and jerky. "Sucks to be alone on New Year's."

"Lucy, I..."

"Don't feel bad, Jake. It's not your fault and I hope you know that I'm not mad at you. I want you to be happy and..."

"Lucy, be quiet! I'm trying to tell you that I'm happy with you! I want to be with you!"

"You can't," she wailed. "You need to have kids, and what if I can't give you that?"

Jake moved toward Lucy and wrapped his hands around hers. He pulled her over toward the couch and settled her into the seat before sitting next to her.

"Listen to me, Luce. I love you. I know you want to be all noble, but I'm not letting you break up with me. Yes, I needed to know about the kids thing, but knowing doesn't change the way I feel about you. I didn't kiss you that first night because I was thinking about genetic compatibility. I kissed you because, well, you're you and you're funny and beautiful and I couldn't help myself."

"But, what if..."

He squeezed her hands tightly. "Don't what if. The 'what if' doesn't matter. We just have to focus on now. Right now, I want to kiss you and love you and ring in the New Year with the person I plan to be with for as long as possible. There are no guarantees, Lucy. We have to take things as they come."

He kissed her, tears and all. Lucy loved him more, if that was even possible. When they pulled apart, she sniffled a bit. "Maybe we can get a dog," she offered.

Jake smiled, full on dimples. "Why don't we start with the New Year and see where we go from there."

"I think it's still the old year in California."

"Good. Then I can give you a midnight kiss."

"Oh, I think you'll get more than a kiss," Lucy teased. Her heart seemed whole again. Nothing had hurt as badly as not being with Jake, but now that he was here, she didn't feel that emptiness.

"Anything to get you out of those ugly sweatpants," he joked and pulled her in for another kiss.

* * *

On January 3rd, Lucy got to meet Jake's parents at the retirement party. She was introduced as his girlfriend and the pressure was on. Now that they were official, there would always be questions about when they were getting married. Once her family got wind of the relationship, her mother would be asking when to expect a grandchild. Lucy would share her medical diagnosis in due time. It was enough to just focus on the moment with Jake. As he'd said, they'd have to wait until they tried to see how things went in that department. Until then, there was no sense worrying about it.

The meeting with Jake's parents went well. His mother eyed her carefully, like she was assessing Lucy's suitability. It might have bothered Lucy before, but she was just too relieved to be at Jake's side to really care. It was fairly clear that she adored Jake, so Lucy hoped that would be enough to win over his mother.

Claudia was around making sure everything went smoothly. Lucy thought her friend looked a little tired, but when she offered to help, she got shooed away. She'd make sure to check on Claudia after the party. Until then, she needed to powder her nose and get back to Jake.

In the washroom, she finished her business and went to wash her hands and fix her makeup. She was adding lipstick when she heard a groan from one of the stalls.

"Dammit!" a woman growled. "Does anyone out there have a tampon?"

Lucy quickly scrounged around her purse. She found one and offered it over the top of the stall. She got a relieved "Thanks" through the door. Getting her period so often made her come prepared. She usually had to have something on her just in case. As she made her way out of the restroom, the thought occurred that she actually hadn't had a period since her doctor's appointment, three weeks ago. It probably didn't mean anything, but her heart skipped a beat. She knew she couldn't read so much into it, but for a few seconds, it gave her a little bit of hope.

* * *

Two weeks later, as she stared down at the little stick with the bright blue plus sign, she was feeling more than a little bit of hope. After waiting for a period that didn't want to show, she'd called her doctor. Dr. Heath had suggested she wait a bit more time and take a test to confirm any results.

Now, here they were, crammed into her small apartment bathroom.

Jake looked at Lucy, a smug grin on his face. "I knew I had super sperm." His chest puffed out with pride. Lucy wanted to throw her arms around him and kiss him. But there was a small part of her that was too scared to believe what all the results were telling them.

"Maybe they're all broken."

At those whispered words, Jake turned to Lucy and waved his arms around the small room, acknowledging the empty pregnancy boxes littering the countertop. "Ten tests can't all be wrong. You're pregnant, Lucy. Correction. *We're* pregnant."

She nodded and a few tears slid down her cheeks. It was true. She was going to have a baby. "Maybe you really do have super sperm," she told him as he wrapped his arms around her, hugging her tightly.

As they stood there, enjoying the moment, Lucy silently thought about how they'd gotten so lucky. In the end, there was really only one thing that made sense. She'd have to thank the Christmas lights.

Thanks to you, our Reader.

Thank you for buying and reading our Christmas anthology.

A year ago our writing group was becoming, well, sluggish. We'd encourage each other, and we'd talk a lot about the writing business and we'd have an occasional speaker to energize us. But writing? Not so much.

Until one day when one of us said, "Why don't we write an anthology and publish an e-book?"

"Yes!" we said enthusiastically. But secretly we each felt doubts. Could we meet a deadline? Would everyone participate? Would stories written under pressure be any good?

We found to our delight that writing was much like exercising: You tend to do more of it if you have to answer to someone else. And, actually doing it made us feel great. Each of us met the deadlines, love each others' stories, and feel great pride in our accomplishment.

All that remains is to please readers. Like you. We hope we did.

Thanks again!
Bluestockings

About the Authors

Christine Wingate is the author of various e-books, including *His Escape Artist*. With a love for 70's culture – she owns both a gold and white disco boots. While several of her book heroes are bodyguards, at the time of this writing Christine does not yet have one in her employ. But if and when she does hire one, odds are good applicants will be asked to demonstrate their ability to tolerate disco and 70's soft rock tunes.

Susan Craig lives with her husband -- in a house they gutted and remodeled together. It comes as no surprise, then, that her life as an author grew out of a desire to do something completely new. With a doctorate in neuroscience, her "day job" is complex, busy and interesting, but "mostly factual." So she enjoys opportunities to create fictitious stories of love and romance purely from her imagination.

Jeanne Kern's life became a romance novel when she met husband Rich online and moved to Nebraska with scaredy cat Boo Radley. Happily retired from teaching high school in Texas, she serves on too many committees and boards and is trying to learn to say no so she can devote more time to writing. See her website for news about her travels, acting career, and e-book *Destination: Love and Whales*.

LK Lien has worked as a waitress, in a bank, as a photojournalist, a writer and an editor. As a child, she read every fairy tale book in the library, over and over and over. As an adult, she still loves the fairy tales shining in romance books.

Karyn Cole has been a fan of romance since a charming Prince's kiss woke Sleeping Beauty. (As a grownup she decided to see what science could teach her and discovered that chemistry didn't just happen in a laboratory. A good romance story lets a reader experience the chemistry between characters.) Now, Karyn writes romance where the Princess doesn't always need a princely rescue, but isn't opposed to the kissing part. Drop her a note at karyncoleromance@gmail.com.

BJ Akin has found that writing stories is almost as much fun as telling them. During her life of living in the Nebraska Sandhills, she experienced things that anyone in their right mind would never attempt or be dared into doing! But that never seemed to stop her. Drawing on her love of this region -- and the people who live there -- she shows that life even in the "olden days" still had its excitement…and romance.